10.95

The Ice Cream Bucket Effect

by
Richard Thompson

The Caitlin Press
Prince George, British Columbia
1993

All rights reserved. No part of this book may be reproduced in any form by any means without the written permission of the publisher, except by a reviewer, who may quote passages in a review.

The Caitlin Press
P.O. Box 2387, Station B
Prince George, B.C. V2N 2S6
Canada

The Caitlin Press would like to acknowledge the financial support of the Canada Council and British Columbia Cultural Fund.

The Talking Meter is reprinted with permission from *IF ONLY. . . . A Compendium of Entrepreneurial Near Misses,* by Gary Cruikshank.

Canadian Cataloguing in Publication Data
Thompson, Richard, 1951-
    The Ice Cream Bucket Effect

    ISBN 0-920576-44-3
    I. Title.
PS8589.H5313 1993   C813'.54   C93-091455-5
PR9199.3.T49613 1993

Cover Design by Gaye Hammond
Typeset by Vancouver Desktop Publishing Centre
Printed in Canada

The Ice Cream Bucket Effect
is dedicated to
Nan

Books by Richard Thompson

For Children:
Jenny's Neighbours
Sky Full of Babies
Foo
I Have to See This
The Last Story, the First Story (novel)
Draw-and-Tell
Gurgle, Bubble, Splash
Effie's Bath
Zoe and the Mysterious 'X'
Sky Full of Babies
  (cassette tape; three stories read by the author)
Zoe and the Mysterious 'X'
  (cassette tape; three stories read by the author)
Jesse of the Night Train
Frog's Riddle and Other Draw-and-Tell Stories
The Last Story, the First Story
  (cassette tape; abridged version of the novel read by the author)
Magee and the Lake Minder
Tell Me One Good Thing
  (six bedtime stories and six poems)
Jill and the Jogero
Thistle Broth
Don't be Scared, Eleven

For Adults:
The Gas Tank of My Heart
  (The Caitlin Press)

Contents

The Drew Drop Inn   1

Mobile Home   7

Hoopla   16

The Visiting Dignitary   25

Rock Salt   33

Epitaph for a Juggling Poet   38

The New Snow Dance   45

Leaning into the Wind   49

The Ghost in the Garbage Can   55

The Fortune Cookie God Speaks   66

The Trotter Family Cookbook   73

Egg Nog   84

Toad Spring   91

Crossing South   95

The Talking Meter   103

The Ice Cream Bucket Effect   106

The Rambler   115

Games of Chance   124

The Bent Owl of Quarter Mile River   131

The Dew Drop Inn

THISTLES ARE GROWING UP through the floor boards now. Most of the paint is gone off the siding, but you can still see that it was painted white at one time — white with black trim around the windows and the doors. The screen is gone from the screen door, and you can just barely make out the words "Coca Cola" on the two bits of twisted tin either side of the door. The name of the place is still there in ghost letters on the old plywood sign — The Dew Drop Inn. Weeds as high as your waist are growing all around the walls, and the outhouse is lying on its side. Not much left of The Dew Drop Inn now, but it was a going concern for a while. It never was a big place, only two painted plywood booths in front by the window and a counter across the back. Along the counter there were four of those spin top kind of stools — chrome with red plastic seats — bolted to the floor. And there was a glass fronted pie case hanging on the back wall above the hole where Ma would pass the food out from the kitchen. That was about all. At lunch time, though, both booths were full and someone was perched on each of the stools. Often as not, someone would have dragged a couple of chairs out of the kitchen and would have a plate of cabbage rolls balanced in his lap, or someone else would have grabbed a Coke box and pulled it up to one of the booths where, with a bit of pushing and shoving, he could find a place to set his plate.

One day late in the winter, a man came into the café. He wasn't the kind of customer that Ma was used to seeing in The Dew Drop Inn. He was wearing a suit and a top coat instead of coveralls and an oily canvas jacket. He had on a felt hat which he took off instead of a tin one that he kept on.

"Mrs. Trotter?" he said.

Ma wiped her hands on her apron and pushed her fingers through her hair.

"That's right," she said.

"My name is Willamson. Tom Williamson. From Edmonton." He stuck out his hand. Ma noticed that there was no grease under his fingernails and the thumbnail wasn't all black where he'd whacked it with a ball peen hammer.

Ma wiped her pudgy hands on her apron again and stuck out the right one. Williamson grabbed hold of it and shook it. When he let go, Ma wiped it once more.

"Piece of pie?" she said.

"Thank you," said Williamson. "Flapper pie if you have any left." He looked around like he couldn't figure what to do next.

"Sit anywhere you like," said Ma. "Coffee?"

The man from Edmonton sat down at the counter and watched Ma as she took the flapper pie out of the glass fronted pie case and cut a wedge. He nodded when she set it down on the counter. Ma went to pour a cup of coffee.

By the time she'd got the coffee, Williamson had hunked off the point and was chewing away with a tiny, sweet smile and graham cracker crumbs on his lips. Ma had never actually seen anybody CHEW flapper pie before.

Williamson teased a paper napkin out of the holder and wiped his mouth.

"It's good," he said, cocking an eyebrow at the pie, "Every bit as good as I've been led to believe."

"Thank you," said Ma.

He pushed the plate away.

"What's your special today, Mrs. Trotter?"

"Corned beef hash," said Ma, "There's a bit left."

"I'll have that," said the man, "And another cup of coffee when you have a minute."

The lunch rush was over so Ma didn't have any hash ready hot, but she got the bowl out of the fridge and spooned a generous portion onto the grill.

Someone was banging on the outside of the kitchen wall.

"Who's doing that banging, Honey?" Ma said to her oldest daughter. Honey was sitting on the counter with her legs dangling down, chewing gum and reading one those religious pamphlets that Ma's sister, Florence, was always sending from Edmonton.

Ma put a plate down on the counter. She peeled off a lettuce leaf and laid it on the plate just so.

"Do you believe this stuff that Auntie Flo keeps sending, Mom?" Honey waved the sheets of newsprint around.

"Flo's got her own ideas about God and . . . what IS that pounding noise?"

"Someone's pounding on something, I guess." Honey put down Aunt Flo's religious pamphlet and picked up a *True Romance Magazine* instead.

Ma put a tomato slice on the lettuce leaf. She stirred the hash around. The pounding noise kept up the whole time.

All of a sudden, there was a terrific caterwauling from outside.

"What in heaven's name! Honey, look after the hash. When it's hot take it to the man at the counter. And give him some more coffee."

Ma ran out the door, skittered across the icy back step, and danced on her toes along the path toward the outhouse.

When she rounded the corner she saw her three year old, Patrick, standing with his arms stretched out against the back wall balanced on an empty Coke bottle crate. His older brother, Andrew, was standing there with the meat tenderizing hammer in his hand.

Now Ma could see that the sleeves of little Patrick's snow suit had been tacked to the wall with a couple dozen fat-headed roofing nails. Patrick was yelling and water was squirting out of his eyes.

"Andrew Trotter!" Ma hollered. "What are you doing to your brother?"

"I'm crucifying him, Ma," said Andrew. And he kicked the box out from under his baby brother's feet.

Patrick dropped about six inches, but the roofing nails held, and he was left hanging there, banging the heels of his rubber boots against the wall and screaming blue murder.

"Get in the house!" Ma barked, and Andrew went.

Ma unzipped the snowsuit and lifted Patrick out, leaving the snowsuit hanging on the wall like the skin of some tiny dead red animal.

When she when storming back into the kitchen with Patrick shivering on her hip, Honey said to her, "Ma, that guy out there wants to talk to you."

"Put that book down and look after your little brother!" Ma plunked Patrick on the counter next to Honey. As she turned to go, she saw the pamphlet from her sister Flo sitting there. She picked it up and looked at it a moment. Sure enough, there was a drawing in greenish ink of Jesus nailed up to a greenish cross. She shook her head, crumpled up the paper and headed out to the front to see what the man from Edmonton wanted. On the way, she saw Andrew's left foot sticking out from behind a sack of potatoes and noted the fact for future reference.

"Honey said you wanted to talk to me?" She didn't sound all that friendly. After the crucifixion business, she wasn't inclined to think particularly kindly of things from Edmonton.

"Mrs. Trotter," said Tom Williamson, "I have just finished a plate of the best corned beef hash that I've ever eaten. . . ."

And, of course, the rest is history. Tom Williamson moved the whole family to Edmonton and set Ma up in the restaurant business, thus launching what has come to be known in culinary history as The Home Cooking Movement. Stews in New York, Hash It Over in San Francisco, Fried or Baked in Calgary — all those places grew up after The Dew Drop Inn . . . they used the same name for the place in Edmonton . . . they all opened after the Dew Drop Inn got to be so famous.

Ma had a cooking show on the radio for a while and you could write in for a copy of that week's recipe. And then when TV came in, Williamson bought Ma a new pair of false teeth and she went on the TV every Thursday afternoon at four o'clock to cook cabbage rolls or dough gods or a denver omelet. Ma got to be a big star, and thistles started poking up through the floor of the little café on the rise overlooking Jackfish Lake.

But, hey, you know that's not the way it happened really. I made most of that up. A fellow did come into the café the day Andrew nailed Patrick to the back wall of the kitchen. And he did look like he might be from Edmonton. But when Ma came back in from rescuing the baby, the man from Edmonton was gone.

Ma's husband, Marvin, was sitting at the counter drinking a cup of coffee, and Andrew was sitting beside him wearing his dad's tin hat.

"I didn't put the nails right through him, Mom," said Andrew in a voice that echoed just the tiniest bit inside the tin hat.

"Go in the back," said Ma in a gruff voice. She didn't want Andrew to see her laughing. Crucifying your brother is a serious business.

"Those kids," she said, "they're going to be the death of me. You know what Andrew did? He nailed Patrick to the back wall."

"He got the idea from those papers your sister keeps sending."

Ma poured herself a cup of coffee. She leaned her elbows on the counter across from her husband and cuddled her fingers around the cup.

"I don't suppose nailing kids to walls is a common practice in Edmonton," she said, "but taking everything into account, I think Devlin would be a better idea."

They'd been talking a lot lately about how — now Andrew was going to have to start school soon, and the rig was going to be moving north in a few weeks — maybe they should sell the trailer and move the family into Edmonton or maybe find a place to park the trailer in some little town. Devlin seemed a good enough little town, and it was close to where the rig would be working for a few months anyway.

"Devlin's fine with me," said Marvin.

Two weeks later the Dew Drop Inn closed its doors for good.

Mobile Home

U P TILL THE TIME THAT Fudgie was old enough to go to school, Ma and the kids followed Marvin around the Vast Northern Prairie wherever the geologists and seismic crews found signs of oil. Every time they moved, Marvin would hire a guy who had a truck with a fifth wheel. They'd hooked onto the trailer, Ma would tie the cupboard doors closed and off they'd go.

They'd park the trailer with the other trailers a hundred yards or so from the rig, hook the oil barrel up to the heater, and they'd be home again. More often than not, home was a square patch of mud carved out of the bush miles from the nearest bit of civilization. It was nice for Marvin to have his family right close by when he climbed down off the derrick and closed the dog house door behind himself at the end of a twelve hour shift, but it was clear that when Fudgie started school the family's gypsy days would have to end. In May of the year Fudgie turned six, they parked the trailer on the bare stretch of gravel between the curling rink and the hotel in Devlin, a village half way between Big Prairie and Novalley. They hooked the oil barrel up to the heater and ran a line from the light pole to the electrical hook-up . . . and they were home.

Mobile homes were a common enough kind of accommodation in that country, but the Trotter's mobile home was unique. From the outside it looked like a freight van slung low to the ground with a jog up at the front where it hooked onto the fifth wheel. And at one time it had been just that — a freight van.

Someone who was handy with a saw and a hammer — not Marvin; Marvin didn't even own a saw — someone had cut holes for windows, insulated and sheeted the inside walls and built in cupboards and a bed that folded down at night. He'd built a little bedroom in the jog at the front. There wasn't much headroom, but there were two bunk beds on one wall and another bed that folded down from the wall on the other side, and there was a little table built under the window at the front. That little room was where the kids slept. There was a cubicle for the chemical toilet and a space for the oil heater. Marvin had been meaning to get someone to build a porch so they'd have a little extra storage space, but he hadn't gotten around to it yet.

As it turned out, Marvin and Ma chose a particularly fortunate spot to park the trailer. Sitting at the table, you could look out the window and see, less that a hundred yards away, the glowing "Ladies and Escorts" sign shining above the door to the beer parlour of the Devlin Hotel. When Marvin came home from the rig on a short change or a long change, he'd take off his greasy coveralls, put on a clean shirt and escort his lady across to the hotel.

"If you need us," Ma would say, "you come and ask Mr. Bowen to find us." Mr. Bowen was the owner of the hotel, and if he wasn't at the front desk he was usually close enough to hear the bell when Fudgie rang. He'd look grumpy when Fudgie asked him to call his mom, but he'd do it, and eventually the door would open and beery laughter and smoke would come wafting out, and Ma would be there to deal with whatever crisis needed dealing with. Sometimes, if the party looked like going on past bed time, Ma would get Sandra Miller to come and stay with the boys.

One summer afternoon, Marvin and the crew arrived in town

feeling hungry and thirsty. Ma fed them potato salad and cold sliced ham and banana cream pie. That took care of the hungry, and then it was time to do something about the thirsty. Sandra Miller came to stay with the boys.

At about the same time that Ma was dishing up the potato salad in Devlin, sixty miles away in Big Prairie, Wayne Watkins, the short half of White Line Moving and Storage was loading the last of the Richter family's thousand and one boxes of household what-nots into the moving van. Normally, he would have been past Fox Creek by that time, but he'd spent the morning trying to figure out why the engine was making that strange clicking noise. Normally too, Harve Moody, the tall half of the company, would have been there to help, but he was attending his grandfather's funeral that day, so Wayne was on his own. But he was almost done now, and if he pushed it, he'd still be in Edmonton by morning, which would give him time — barely — to unload in time to pick up that load of tractor parts at MasseyFerguson in the afternoon. About the time Marvin and Ma and the crew headed out the door and across to the beer parlour, Wayne closed and latched the doors on the van and climbed into the cab of the truck.

Sandra Miller was standing in the yard yelling, "Fudgie! Patrick! It's time to come in now and get ready for bed!" Marvin was waggling his fingers at the bartender to signal for another round of beer. Fudgie and Patrick were busy ignoring the babysitter. They were using a butcher knife to chop down a small poplar tree for their log cabin and they wanted to get it done before dark. And Wayne was worrying about the hot, greasy smell wafting through the cab as the truck laboured up the Smokey River hill.

Sandra Miller shrugged her shoulders and went back into the trailer. She picked up the *True Romance Magazine* off the couch and went back to reading a story about an unwed mother of six. Ma told an off-colour joke about a policeman and a cow and Marvin almost choked on his beer. Fudgie stopped hacking at the tree and rubbed his sore muscles. "Chopping trees is hard work, hey. . . ." said Patrick. And Wayne hoped there was a garage in Devlin, and that the truck would make it that far before it blew up.

There was a garage in Devlin — Wringle's Esso. Wayne breathed a sigh of relief and pulled in beside the gas pumps. Agnes Wringle put down her crochetting and came out from the back to tell him that he could find Ben over at the hotel, but she didn't know how much mechanicking he'd be up to that evening. Wayne drove over to the hotel and parked the van in the red glow of the "Ladies and Escorts" sign.

Wayne found Ben easily enough — he was the only one in the bar wearing welding goggles. Wayne joined the table and bought the mechanic a beer. After Ben had drained the beer, Wayne tugged at his nose and introduced the subject of the engine.

"It started out with a funny ticking noise and now there's a hot, oily smell, and every once in a while a bit of black smoke."

Ben finished his beer, adjusted his goggles and stood up. He followed Wayne out to the truck. He looked under the hood and looked at the big black puddle that had collected in the gravel, and suggested that Wayne unhook the trailer and drive the tractor over to the garage where the light would be better. Once the truck was in the shop, Ben didn't look long before he suggested to Wayne that they might as well go back to the beer parlour, because that truck wasn't going to make it even out to the highway, let alone to Edmonton, and there was nothing he could do about it tonight.

Wayne phoned and left a message at Harve's house and accepted his misfortune with good grace.

Sandra Miller was asleep on the couch with a crochetted afghan pulled up to her chin. Fudgie was asleep on the top bunk, and

Patrick had rolled out of bed and was sleeping under the table. The "Ladies and Escorts" sign had just winked out and the bartender had announced last call. And Harve, reading the message that his wife had written by the telephone, cursed under his breath.

"Wayne phoned," the note said. "Truck broke down in Devlin. Bring other truck."

Harve had been up early to drive to Fort Mellon for the funeral and then all the way home again after — and he didn't feel like driving anymore that night. But if they didn't get there to pick up those tractor parts by the next afternoon, Prairie Schooners would get the next contract. He wrote a note for his wife and left the house.

Sandra Miller was in her own bed and three dollars richer. Fudgie was wrestling with a bear in his dreams. Patrick was back under his quilt. Ma and Marvin were snoring side by side, a cloud of beer fumes hovering above their pillows. Wayne was asleep in Room 101 at the hotel. And Harve was just making the turn by the show hall.

Ten minutes later, Harve was climbing into bed and Wayne was stumbling down the stairs, tucking his shirt in as he went. Ten minutes after that, Wayne had the truck backed up to the wrong trailer and was setting the hitch on the fifth wheel.

Marvin woke up as the trailer started to move, but figured the movement was just the beer. He groaned, turned over and went back to sleep. Fudgie started dreaming that he was a pirate riding out a storm at sea. Patrick fell out of bed again.

Ten minutes later, the Trotter family was on the highway, heading for Edmonton.

Fudgie woke up with the first light and headed for the kitchen which was, in fact, the same room as the livingroom and his parents' bedroom except that it was at the far end and had cupboards and a stove and a fridge. He bounced off the wall once when

Wayne swerved to avoid a pot hole and again a moment later when Wayne swerved the other way to avoid hitting a skunk. Fudgie didn't think much about it though; he often banged into the walls when he first got up — he wasn't much of a morning person.

When his parents' bed was folded down from the wall, it filled all the space between the wall and the couch, so to reach the kitchen, Fudgie had to walk across the bed. He stumbled once and stepped on a part of his dad, causing his dad to flail about wildly in his sleep a moment before flopping back to snore again.

Fudgie got some cornflakes out of the cupboard and a bottle of milk out of the fridge. He got a big bowl and a spoon and settled himself at the table. He filled the bowl with cornflakes, sprinkled on three spoonfuls of sugar and poured on the milk. While he waited for the milk to sog into the cornflakes, he dug his hand down into the box and felt around. Oh good! He'd got there before Patrick! He pulled out his hand and checked the prize — a pair of 3-D glasses with one red cellophane lens and one green cellophane lens! Ma had already explained to them that to get the 3-D book to read with the 3-D glasses you had to send away four box tops and twenty-five cents. Fudgie ripped open the package and put the glasses on. Neat! When he closed his right eye everything looked green! And when he closed his left eye, everything looked red! And when he stood up and looked out the window it looked like he was moving. It looked like he was going about forty miles an hour though Spruce Grove. Wow! Who needed a comic book! These glasses were great!

"Fudgie. . . ." Fudgie turned to see his brother standing beside him. He closed his left eye. Patrick turned a warm shade of red.

"Fudgie," he said, "How come the trailer is moving?"

Fudgie switched eyes and Patrick turned all green, like a little Martian.

"It's the glasses," said Fudgie. "They're 3-D glasses and they make everything look like it's moving."

"But I don't have any glasses. . . ." said Patrick.

"And you can't have mine!" declared Fudgie. "You'll have to wait till Mom opens the next box of cornflakes."

"Fudgie," said Patrick, "How come when you wear the glasses, I can see the trailer moving?"

"Huh?" said Fudgie. He took off the glasses and looked out the window. Patrick was right—even without the glasses on it, looked like they were moving. And that could only mean one thing. . . .

"I think we're moving," said Fudgie.

"Where are we moving to?" asked Patrick.

Fudgie looked out the window just in time to catch a glimpse of a billboard advertising a car dealership and his eye caught the word "Edmonton."

"Maybe we're moving to Edmonton," he ventured.

"I guess Dad's rig had to move again," said Patrick.

"I guess," said Fudgie. And the two brothers sat in companionable silence watching the landscape slide by and eating cornflakes.

Wayne stopped for gas and directions at a gas station on the edge of the city and as he was walking back to the truck after paying the bill and using the facilities, he stopped walking and looked at the trailer. There was something not quite right about that trailer, he thought. There was a window in the side of the trailer that shouldn't be there. And there were two faces looking at him out the window. One of the faces had one green eye and one red eye.

"What the hey!" he said to himself. He looked around to make sure he was looking at the right truck. That was the only freight van parked at the gas station and the sign on the door said "White Line Moving and Storage." . . .

"What the hey!" Wayne said again.

The two faces disappeared from the window and appeared again a moment later at the door.

"Hi!" said the one with the coloured eyes.

"What are you doing in my truck?" said Wayne. He didn't like the way the kid kept closing one eye and then the other like that.

"We're moving to Edmonton," said the other kid. "We used to live in Devlin, but my dad's rig got moved so we're moving to Edmonton."

At the mention of Devlin, the penny dropped. Wayne realized what he'd done. Ten minutes later he was on the road again, heading back toward Devlin. In the fold-down bed in the trailer that Wayne had abandoned in the parking lot, Ma and Marvin were drifting reluctantly toward consciousness. And Fudgie and Patrick were having Root Beer floats in the coffee shop that was attached to the gas station.

Ma and Marvin straggled in a bit later, and over bacon and eggs and black coffee, they reviewed the situation. They knew where they were. And they agreed that they weren't even going to TRY and figure out why they were where they were. But they did have to figure out what they were going to do next.

They didn't have the ready cash to hire a truck with a fifth wheel to take them back to Devlin, and besides, Marvin didn't have time to deal with it; he had to be back at work the next morning. In the end, they decided that Ma would call her sister, Florence, who lived in Edmonton and she and the boys would go stay there for a while. Marvin would hitch-hike back to Devlin and, with any luck, make it in time for work. The next long change, he'd come for them.

With one thing and another, it was late summer before the

family got back to Devlin. They parked the trailer back in front of the curling rink and hooked up the oil barrel again.

A week later, Fudgie picked up his black tin lunch bucket and kissed his mom good-bye. He went out the door and headed across the space of gravel to where a bunch of kids were already gathered in front of the hotel waiting for the school bus. Out in the bush away to the north-east somewhere, Marvin picked up his lunch pail and headed down the steel stairs from the dog house at the end of the graveyard shift.

Ma and Patrick, each wearing a pair of 3-D glasses, sat watching out the window as Fudgie climbed onto the school bus. They waved. As the bus pulled out, the "Ladies and Escorts" sign over the beer parlour door winked on, and the sun came peeking around the corner of the hotel.

Hoopla

WITH THE MEN IT MIGHT BE horseshoe pitching, with the women it might be jam making, with the kids it'd be jacks or mumbly peg or spitting for distance, but it seemed like the folks in Devlin, big or little, were forever taking on the folks in Twisty River in some kind of contest. So it was pretty well inevitable that, once Morrison's General Store in Devlin got in a shipment of hoola hoops and Withey's General Store in Twisty River got in a bunch a week later, and once a fair number of kids in both towns learned how to use them, someone would challenged someone to a hoola hooping contest.

Agnes Wringle bragged to Edna Hopkins about how her girl, Elaine, could twirl one hoop around her middle and a second around her arm at the same time, and that's all it took. Sunday, June 11, the best hoola-er in Devlin would go wiggle to wiggle against the best hooper in Twisty River.

Since Elaine could do two hoops and Edna Hopkins' girl, Gayle, could keep it up for hours and hours and never get tired, Agnes and Edna decided that the contest would be in three parts: Most Hoops At One Time, Endurance, and Free Style.

But the fact of the matter was, Elaine Wringle was not the best hoola-er in Devlin, nor was Gayle Hopkins the best in Twisty River. During the preliminary rounds both Elaine and Gayle were eliminated early on.

A week before the big day, the finalists were decided; on June 11 it would be little Patrick Trotter from Devlin against Helen Gunderson from Twisty River. Agnes was disappointed that Elaine wouldn't be swaying her hips to the greater glory of Devlin, but she had to agree that Patrick was the right and proper one to represent the town.

"He can do five at a time," she bragged to Mrs. Morrison, "one around his middle, one around each arm, one around his neck and one around his left ankle!"

Mrs. Morrison bragged right back, "He was outside the store this morning hoola hooping and skipping rope at the same time."

Patrick's older brother, Andrew, plunked a package of Spangles on the counter and fished in his jeans for a dime.

"That's not all he can do, Mrs. Morrison," he said proudly. "Patrick can climb up the rope into our tree house hand over hand WHILE he's hoola hooping! Heck, most kids can't even climb up there when they're NOT hoola hooping!"

On the afternoon of Tuesday, June 6, Andrew was working on the paint-by-number picture that his Aunt Florence had sent from Edmonton — a lighthouse by the ocean with big waves crashing on the rocks. He had just finished off the last of the number fourteen and was opening up the number fifteen when Patrick came in. While Andrew was trying to wrestle the lid off the jar of number fifteen, Patrick got out a loaf of Wonder Bread and the margarine.

"Boy, am I ever hungry," he said. "I've been hoola hooping since breakfast."

That day Patrick had started hoola hooping right after breakfast. He'd hoola hooped to the bus stop, up the steps onto the bus and all the way to school. He'd hoola hooped through "The Lord's Prayer," "O Canada," and spelling. He'd hoola hooped through lunch and reading. And he was still hoola hooping when they got on the bus to come back home.

"Finally got tired out, did you?" said Andrew. Ah! The lid was loose. Number fifteen looked good — bright red, smooth and glossy!

"Got hungry," said Patrick. "A person can't eat and hoola hoop at the same time. Hey, where's the ketchup, Andy? Are we out of ketchup! Who ate all the ketchup! How am I supposed to make a ketchup sandwich if I don't have any ketchup!"

"Have a mustard sandwich then," said Andrew.

"Mustard sandwiches taste like pig manure!" Patrick whined. "I want ketchup!"

"Alright," said Andrew. "You can have mine."

"You have some ketchup?"

"I was going to use it to paint the stripes on the lighthouse, but if you want it you can have it." Andrew held out the jar of red paint to his brother.

"That's not ketchup," Patrick said. "That's paint."

"No, it's ketchup. This is an edible paint-by-number set. All the colours are different kinds of food. See number five was gravy. And number eleven was mustard. Go ahead. Have a little taste. You'll see."

Suspiciously, Patrick stuck just the end of one baby finger into the paint jar. He licked off the dab of red paint.

Andrew grinned. Now was time for his brother to start spitting and cursing and wiping his tongue on his sleeve and going "Ack! Ack! Pitooey!" But Patrick saw that little grin on his brother's face and there was no way that he was going to give Andrew the satisfaction of hearing him going "Ack! Ack! Pitooey!" and spitting and cursing.

"Mmmm. . . ." said Patrick. "Thank you, Andy."

And as cool as a frog in a dishpan, he took that jar of number fifteen over to the counter, scooped out the paint with a butter knife and smeared it on his slice of Wonder Bread. Then with a look of profound satisfaction on his face, he ate that red paint sandwich right down to the crusts. Patrick never ate crusts.

That was Tuesday afternoon. Somewhere in the middle of Wednesday night, Patrick started puking and moaning and holding his stomach. When he was still moaning on Thursday morning, Ma asked Agnes Wringle if she'd drive her and Patrick into Big Prairie to the doctor.

"It came on really sudden," said Ma. "He was fine at supper time, and then it just came on. I don't know what it could be. . . ."

Andrew knew, though. He'd poisoned his little brother. He'd made him eat oil paint and now his little brother was going to die. It was his fault.

"I promise, God," Andrew muttered to himself as the Wringle's car disappeared down the street, "if You save Patrick, I'll never paint another paint-by-number picture again."

Andrew wasn't able to concentrate much at school that day, what with thinking about his brother being dead, and wondering if he'd have to help carry the coffin, and thinking about how it would be kind of nice having the bedroom all to himself, and imagining the worms eat his poor brother's guts out and fretting that they might find out and put him in jail for murder and thinking about what colour could he make the stripes on the lighthouse now that all the bright red was used up, and remembering how much he used to like Patrick when they weren't fighting about something and thinking maybe he should run away before it was too late. And with all that thinking he only got four out of ten right on his spelling test, and now he had one more thing to worry about.

"You don't worry, Andrew," Ma told him when he got home that afternoon. "Patrick is going to be alright. The doctor says he's got chronic appendicitis. He'll be fine in a couple of days."

"Well, you can say don't worry, Ma," said Agnes Wringle, "but what about the hoola hooping contest? Who's going to take Patrick's place?"

Andrew's body started to tingle all over. A wave of hot swept down from the top of his head to his toes. He knew! He knew what he had to do to make up for nearly killing his little brother!

"I'll do it, Mrs. Wringle!" he declared. "I'll take Patrick's place!"

"But . . . but you're not much good, Andrew," said Mrs. Wringle. "I mean, you're smart, and you paint nice pictures, but you're not much good at hoola hooping."

"I know," said Andrew, "but Patrick is my brother, and I'm his brother. We're brothers."

Well, Agnes Wringle couldn't argue with that.

"Alright, Andrew," she said. "But you better start practicing."

Andrew was a long time getting to sleep that night. At the time, it had seemed like a good idea, but now it seemed like a really bad idea. He wasn't sure which was worse — worrying about a dead brother or worrying about losing the hoola hooping contest and getting laughed at and having all the grown ups mad at him for disgracing the whole town. Well, it was too late now, his brother wasn't dead, and he'd gone and opened his big mouth.

By Saturday afternoon, Andrew had worked himself up to being able to keep one hoola hoop going on each arm, but he had a feeling it wasn't going to be enough. He'd have to count on the Free Style and Endurance sections of the contest.

The contest was held on the ball diamond at the Grindrod Community Hall halfway between Devlin and Twisty River. Agnes Wringle drove Andrew out to the hall.

"Just do your best, Andrew," she said. "That's all you can do."

But Andrew's best wasn't going to be good enough. Twenty minutes into the Endurance section of the contest, Andrew knew that with a painful certainty. The stitch in his side was getting worse with every twirl of that bright yellow hoop. And now he was starting to feel a little dizzy and his stomach was doing a hoola all its own inside him. At the twenty-nine minute mark, Andrew's hoop dropped to the ground, and Andrew staggered to the bleachers and sat with his head drooping between his knees.

Helen Gunderson came over in the break between the Endurance and the Free Style and sat down beside Andrew.

"Would you like a piece of cake, Andrew?" she said, pushing a big slab of Angel Food cake under his nose.

"No thanks," said Andrew. "Maybe later. I don't think I could eat anything right now. . . ."

Now, Andrew hadn't quite worked out what he was going to do during the Free Style, but as he said those words, the words that Patrick had spoken on that fateful Tuesday echoed in his brain: "A person can't hoola hoop and eat at the same time. . . ."

"But if a person COULD!" thought Andrew excitedly. "If a person COULD. . . ."

When the Free Style section was announced a few minutes later, Andrew surprised everyone by stepping forward and volunteering to go first.

He draped his yellow plastic hoop around his neck and gave it a fling. In a moment, the hoop was hoola-ing around his neck in a steady rhythm. With a look of concentration on his face, Andrew walked over to the food table which had been set up in the shade behind the bleachers. Very carefully, he reached down with one hand and picked up a plate of matrimonial squares. He held the plate in his left hand and lifted off one square with his right.

Around, the hoop went. Around, and around and around. Now! Just at the point when the hoop was starting around to the back, Andrew popped the matrimonial square into his mouth. As the hoop went round and round, he chewed and swallowed.

An awed hush fell over the crowd. Andrew took another square off the plate and with perfect timing, threw it into his mouth just as the hoop came swishing by.

The crowd buzzed.

Now Andrew wasn't known as an athlete, but he did possess an almost uncanny ability to bring hand to mouth with unerring accuracy. And calling upon that skill now, he was able, while twirling a hoola hoop around his neck, to consume that whole plate of matrimonial squares, a half a dozen butter tarts, the remains of the Angel Food cake and a quart of Neopolitan ice cream.

By the time he was finished all the Devlinians — and not a few Twisty Riverians — were cheering.

Helen Gundersen had planned to embroider a pansy on a handkerchief while spinning one hoop around her middle and another on her ankle for her Free Style demonstration, but. . . . "You can't do that now, Helen," whispered her mother. "Not after Andrew's performance. You'll have to eat. If Andrew could do it, you can do it."

"But, Mother. . . ."

"Don't 'but Mother' me!" hissed Myrtle Gundersen. "Just do it!"

Well, Helen tried, but if Patrick Trotter says a person can't eat and hoola hoop at the same time, you have to know that it's not an easy thing to do. Within two minutes, Helen had ice cream in her ears, chocolate cake in her hair and tears in her eyes.

"I give up," she wailed. "I can't do it!"

Edna Hopkins and Myrtle Gunderson took Helen off to the

washroom to clean her up a bit before the Most Hoops At One Time part of the contest began.

Andrew took three hoops — his yellow one, a blue one, and Patrick's favourite green one — out to the edge of the parking lot. If he could get just three going at once, he thought, maybe he'd have a chance. Well, he had one going on one arm when he noticed a plume of dust in the west. He got to wondering what it could be, and unable to wonder and whirl at the same time, he dropped the hoop. After that he forgot about the plume of dust and turned his thoughts to the task at hand. When they called him to come for the Most Hoops At One Time, though, he happened to glance westward, and he noticed that the plume of dust was a lot closer now.

He didn't have time to think more about it right then, because he saw that Helen Gunderson was up on the pitcher's mound, and she already had four hoops spinning. She had two going around one leg, one around her middle, and one around her arm. As he watched in amazement, he saw her add in a fifth around her other arm and a sixth around her neck.

Andrew turned away in despair just in time to see Ivan Morrison's pick-up come flying into the parking lot with a plume of dust on its tail. The truck stopped and was immediately lost in a swirling brown cloud. Suddenly, from out of that cloud, Andrew saw a small form taking shape. The ghost of his dead brother was walking toward him across the parking lot! No! Not the ghost of his dead brother! It WAS his dead brother! It was his dead brother! And he was alive! Andrew went running to meet him.

Behind him Andrew could hear the crowd roaring as Helen Gunderson took a bow.

"Patrick," Andrew said, putting his arm around his brother. "How are you feeling? Are you okay?"

Without a word, Patrick took the hoola hoops from his brother and walked toward the pitcher's mound.

As he walked, he put the three hoops around his middle and started them twirling all at once. It took a moment before someone noticed, but soon one person was poking his neighbour and then that neighbour was poking his neighbour and neighbours all around were shaking their heads and exclaiming in whispers.

"How's he doing that?"

"I don't think that's possible!"

"It's amazing!"

Patrick was twirling three hoops around his middle all at once, but what was causing all the comment was the fact that two of the hoops were twirling to the left and the third was twirling to the right.

Patrick picked up another hoop and started it going on his leg. He grabbed another and started it going the other way on his foot. A moment later, he had two going in opposite directions on his neck and four more going on his right arm.

The crowd was too dumbfounded to cheer. They just stood there in the dusty haze of that June afternoon watching in silence as the hoops kept spinning and spinning and spinning.

Finally, Andrew stepped out of the crowd.

"Patrick," he said. "I think you can stop now. I thought you must be really hungry, so I made you a ketchup sandwich."

With a big grin on his face, Patrick Trotter let the hoops drop. As the crowd broke into thunderous applause, he took the ketchup sandwich from his brother and took a great big bite.

The Visiting Dignitary

WHEN DORA RITTER GOT ATTACKED by kidney stones, she got to ride to the hospital in the town ambulance. But that was AFTER the New Totem Days Parade and AFTER the Visiting Dignitary had been and gone. When Ma Trotter'd broken her leg six months earlier, it was a different story. . . .

"Hello, operator? Could you send an ambulance? My mom fell down and broke her leg. Huh? 968 - 107th Avenue. And you better tell them to send an extra guy. My mom is a pretty big woman."

It wasn't quite accurate to call Ma Trotter "big" — she was only about four foot ten high, but she DID weigh well over two hundred pounds.

"I mean . . . she's not tall, but she's really heavy. . . ."

Fudgie hung up the phone and went and sat on the utility room floor by his mom.

"You okay, Mom? I phoned. They're sending the ambulance. Mom," he said, "what were you doing out in the back yard at four o'clock in the morning?"

"I went out to look at the northern lights," said Ma in a tiny, broken voice. "They were really pretty. I tripped coming back to the house and fell down."

She didn't mention that it was Fudgie's hockey stick that she'd tripped over. She didn't want him to feel bad.

The phone rang, and Fudgie went to answer it. It was the Carson's Creek telephone operator.

"This is the Carson's Creek operator calling. Did you call for an ambulance? What town are you calling from? New Totem? Oh, well, that explains it. The driver said there was no 107th Avenue, and I told him yes there was, look again 'cause there's a lady there with a broken leg. He said what the heck was she doing at four o'clock in the morning to break her leg, and I said . . . She was what? Looking at the northern lights? Oh. Well, is she still out there in the back yard? Well, if she can crawl, she couldn't have broken it too bad, I guess . . . Did you say you're calling from New Totem? Well, if it's a different town, that explains it. I'll call the New Totem ambulance then."

"I got connected to the wrong operator," Fudgie explained to his mother. "But she's going to call the ambulance driver here now. You want an aspirin, Mom?"

A few minutes later, the phone rang again.

"This is the Carson's Creek operator calling. The ambulance driver and his wife are out sanding the streets, but the girl who answered the phone said they should be in for breakfast any time now, and she'd give them the message."

The New Totem ambulance driver was Maurice (pronounced More-iss, NOT More-ees!) King. Maurice had the contract to operate the town's fleet of service vehicles which included the ambulance, the snow plow and sand truck, the dog-catching truck, and the garbage truck. The ambulance was an old hearse that the mayor had picked up cheap when a funeral home in Edmonton went bankrupt. Maurice was in the process of painting it white, but so far he'd only got as far as the giving it a first sanding and plugging some of the bigger dents with body putty. One beat-up half ton pick-up served as snow plow, sand truck, garbage truck, and dog-catching truck. In the summer, Maurice put an old camper on the back to put stray dogs in and to use on fishing trips on the weekends. In the winter, he rigged a blade on the front and the camper came off so he could put a load of sand in the back. Dark winter mornings you'd see Maurice and his wife, Lyla, out with the truck, Maurice driving and working the plow, Lyla in the back with a scoop shovel throwing sand on the icy spots. As a sideline, Maurice operated the Chinook Taxi Company — one 1963 four-door Ford.

Both Fudgie and Ma fell into a fitful sleep on the utility room floor, so neither of them knew for sure how much later it was that Maurice came pounding on the door.

"Sorry I took so long getting here, Ma," he said. "Lyla and me were out doing the roads. Maureen gave me the message as soon as I got in. She said you broke your leg?"

"Yes," said Fudgie. "My mom fell down. . . ."

"Let's have a look," said Maurice. "Hm . . . I'd say that break was closer to the ankle than the leg. No, I'd have to say, this isn't a broken leg at all. . . ."

"Can you still take her to the hospital?" asked Fudgie shyly.

"Of course! Of course!" said Maurice. "Just have to get her into the truck."

"Aren't you the ambulance driver?" asked Fudgie.

"I'm the everything driver," said Maurice. "But Maureen said it was an emergency. I didn't want to take time to switch the battery over, so I brought the sand truck."

Maurice only had one battery that he switched from the half ton to the ambulance to the taxi as the need arose.

"I could go back and get the ambulance, Ma," he offered. "And I could bring Lyla and Maureen to help carry. . . ."

"Don't bother," said Ma. "I don't want to be carted off in a hearse just yet anyway. Just back the truck up to the step, and I can make my own way. Fudgie, go and get a couple of blankets. . . ."

And so it was that Ma Trotter rode off to the Sisters of Mercy Hospital in the back of the New Totem sand, garbage, and dog-catching truck early on a winter's morning. But late in the summer of the same year, when Dora Ritter had the attack of kidney stones, she rode to the hospital in style. By then Maurice King had a battery for each the three vehicles in his fleet, plus an extra one on the shelf in his garage. All thanks to The Visiting Dignitary.

The first Saturday of July was always the day of the big New Totem Days Parade, and that year — the year Ma Trotter broke her leg — that year the parade was more spectacular than ever. There were the regular floats from the 4-H club and the Gopher Hole Pub, and there were the decorated bicycles and the horses. There was a combine and a baler from Hunter Farm Equipment and a D-9 Cat on a flat-bed truck courtesy of Bolger Bros. Construction. There were the New Totem Queen and her Princesses, and the candy stripers pushing a hospital bed. But that year, there was something extra — that year there was a VISITING DIGNITARY.

It just happened that Colonel Sanders was going to be in town on the first Saturday in July that year to open the new Kentucky Fried Chicken store next to the Thrift Shop. The minute Mayor Walsh heard that, he fired off a letter to Fried Chicken headquarters in Kentucky and put in a bid to have the Colonel participate in the parade. Fried Chicken headquarters agreed on behalf of The Colonel, and Mayor Walsh set the wheels in motion.

On the morning of the parade, Mayor Walsh, in his best brown suit, was standing watching Maurice King, in his best white shirt and string tie, moving the battery from the taxi to the dog-catching truck.

"I'm sorry about that, Mayor," said Maurice. "The way she was burning oil, it was only a matter of time before she blew up. But it was plain bad luck she picked today to do it."

"Well, if you'd have got the ambulance painted we could have used that," said the Mayor, "but the way it is, it still looks more like a hearse than an ambulance. We can't be driving a Visiting Dignitary in the parade in a second-hand hearse."

"It'll have to be the dog-catching truck then," said Maurice.

"What about the girls?" said the Mayor.

As soon as he'd got official word from Fried Chicken Headquarters saying that the Colonel had agreed to ride in the parade, the Mayor had organized a contest to choose some beautiful girls to ride in the parade with him — Miss Breast and her two attendants, Miss Thigh, and Miss Wing. Olive Rigley beat out eight other local beauties to be chosen Miss Breast. The two runners-up, Georgina Wood and Rena Boulanger, got to be Miss Thigh and Miss Wing respectively.

"There won't be room in the cab for The Colonel and you and all three girls."

"How about the girls ride up on top of the camper," suggested Maurice. "The crowd'll be able to see them better up there anyway. . . ."

Maurice picked up Colonel Sanders at the airport in the dog-catching truck and drove him straight down to the marshalling area in front of the Civic Arena.

"Honored to meet, you, Colonel," said the Mayor. "I'd like to introduce you to Miss Breast, and Miss Thigh, and Miss Wing." The three girls were dressed in brown leotards and feathered head-dresses. Their leotards were all bespangled with thirteen different colours of sequins to represent the thirteen secret herbs and spices in the Colonel's recipe. The girls all curtsied to the Visiting Dignitary.

"They'll be riding up on top of the camper and waving and throwing pieces of chicken to the crowd. Now don't worry, Colonel, we're not expecting you to pay for the chicken. That's all paid for out of petty cash. All you got to do is wave and smile."

So the New Totem dog-catching truck inched its way up Centre Street behind the decorated bicycles with Maurice King at the wheel and The Colonel sitting in his white suit on the passenger side, smiling and waving.

As they turned the corner by Totem Gifts, Maurice gave a toot on the horn, and Miss Breast popped the top off a bucket of succulent chicken. As the parade passed the Marshal Wells store and the Coronation Theatre with the secret aroma perfuming the breeze, Miss Thigh and Miss Wing started throwing drumsticks to the hungry crowd.

By the time they reached Bevin Williams Junior Secondary, they were down to their last bucket of chicken, and a whole new contingent had joined the New Totem Days Parade. Maurice looked in the rear-view mirror to see a pack of about forty dogs — big ones, small ones, curly ones, mangy ones — following the truck.

"Well, Colonel," said Maurice, "if just half those dogs can find themselves paying work, your new place is going to make you a lot of money. . . ."

An hour after they'd left the Civic Arena, they were back again.

"I'm just going to make one quick stop before we call quits to this parade, Colonel," said Maurice.

Maurice went right on past the Civic Arena and down the street past the Arena Grocery. And all forty dogs followed right along behind.

"Don't worry, girls," Maurice hollered out the window. "I'm just going to swing by my place. I'll have you back at to the Arena in plenty of time for the barbecue. . . ."

Maurice pulled up in front of the big double doors of his shop.

"You mind getting out and swinging those doors open, Colonel?"

The Colonel slid out of the pick-up and was immediately set upon by a dozen chicken-hungry mongrels. He chased them off a ways with his gold-headed cane and hobbled over to the big double doors. He swung them open.

"Stand right there, Colonel," hollered Maurice, "and be ready to swing those doors shut again. Watch your heads, girls!"

Maurice pulled the truck into the shop next to the ambulance. Immediately, all forty dogs came crowding in behind him, lured on by the aroma of thirteen secret herbs and spices and the sight of those three gigantic pieces of chicken sitting on the roof of the camper. As soon as the last wagging tail was in, Colonel Sanders swung the doors shut.

Hollering over the howling and yapping, Maurice explained to Miss Breast and her two attendants how they should climb down onto the hood of the truck and leap across to the tool bench. From there they crawled out the window and climbed down the wood-pile into the yard. It was a bit of a tight fit for Maurice, but he crawled through, too. Then Maurice, The Visiting Dignitary, and the three pieces of delectable fried chicken walked back to the Civic Arena and the barbecue.

I don't know how The Colonel got back to the airport that

evening, but he must have done, because I saw him on TV the next week, grinning and licking his fingers.

The day after the parade, Maurice issued citations to all forty dogs, and took in more money in fines than he'd made in all the previous three summers that he'd been town dog catcher.

He used the cash to buy three new batteries — now he had one for each of his vehicles plus a spare — and a new shovel for Lyla.

Rock Salt

Rock salt came in two colors — pink and blue. Both tasted the same — salty. And both cost the same — nothing. Farmers put big blocks of the stuff out for their cows to lick, in the theory — I imagine — that grass tastes better with a pinch of salt. Any kid who was shy the price of a bag of potato chips — and who just happened to be passing a farmer's field — could duck through the fence, crack a hunk of rock salt off the block, and be sucking salt for the rest of the afternoon.

Davey Winchester was always shy the price of a bag of potato chips, so when he passed Old John Perkins's north pasture that afternoon, it was natural that he should think to stop and stock up on rock salt.

He slid very carefully between the top strand and the middle strand of barbed wire, ran across to the blue block of salt and chipped off four or five good-sized pieces. Then, for good measure, he ran across to the pink block and chipped off another four or five pieces of the pink kind.

He was sliding very carefully back through the fence with his pants pockets bulging with hunks of rock salt when something grabbed him by the back of his shirt.

"Old Perkins! Old Perkins has got me!" Davey thought.

"Let me go!" he hollered, "I'm going to be late for school!"

He trashed about trying to get loose, and by the time he realized that it was the barbed wire and not Old John Perkins that had hold of him, he was snagged and snagged good.

He hung there on the wire wondering what to do, and he'd been hanging already quite a while when a sideways-walking dog sidled up to him.

The dog sniffed at Davey with his long, ugly nose. He eyed the boy with his pale white eyes. He licked his yellow teeth with his long tongue.

He said — the dog did — he said, "This looks okay to eat."

"NO!" yelped Davey, "You can't eat me!"

"Why not?" said the dog.

"Because . . . because. . . ." said Davey, "because I'm not ready yet. Old John Perkins hung me up to dry, and in a couple of weeks he's going to have some boy jerky. He wouldn't like it if you ate me before I was ready."

The dog sucked at his long yellow teeth and cocked one eye at the boy, "I don't think Old John will miss a bite here and a bite there. Do you?"

"Well, take a bite or two as long as they're small ones," said Davey, "But don't think about eating the bottoms of my feet."

He reached down and pulled off one running shoe. He clutched onto it tight.

"Salted foot bottoms is what Old John likes the best," said the boy, "salted foot bottoms and a big tumbler of cold water. He'll be really mad if you eat his favourite part."

"The foot bottoms, eh?" said the sideways-walking dog, "Just so happens that foot bottoms is what I like best, too!"

And he snatched the shoe out of Davey's hand. The dog hadn't noticed Davey stuffing a couple of big hunks of rock salt down into the toe of the running shoe, and he chomped it down, rock salt and all.

"Whew!" he said. "That is SALTY! Excuse me a minute. . . ."

He sidled off across the pasture at a run. He sidled up to the pump in the middle of Old John Perkins' yard. He stuck his snout under the spout and worked the handle up and down with one hind leg — scree haw! scree haw! scree haw! He pumped and guzzled and guzzled and pumped until the well was dry.

"That's better!" he said. And back he sidled — out to the north pasture where Davey was still hanging on the barbed wire fence.

The sideways-walking dog saw that the boy was clutching his other foot bottom in his two hands, and he chuckled a nasty little chuckle when the boy said to him, "Dog, have an ear, have a couple of fingers, but please don't eat this foot bottom. Think how happy Old John will be chewing on it and drinking a big mug of cool milk."

Now the sideways-walking dog didn't particularly want another salty helping of foot bottom, but he figured he could force himself if it would make Old John Perkins miserable.

So he said, "I can see that that would make him happy, because it's going to make me happy right now. Give me that foot bottom."

The dog grabbed the shoe and chewed it down. You know, of course, that the toe of the shoe was stuffed with hunks of rock salt.

The dog licked his lips and said in kind of a dry gasp, "Whew! That is SALTY! Excuse me a minute. . . ."

He sidled off across the pasture at a run. He sidled up to the pump in the middle of Old John Perkins' yard. He stuck his snout under the spout and worked the handle up and down with one hind leg — scree haw! scree haw! scree haw! But the well was dry.

The dog looked around with desperately thirsty eyes and spotted the milking shed. He sidled over and poked his nose in through the door. There were half a dozen cream cans lined up against the wall. He sidled over and kicked the first one with his hind leg.

The cream can said, "DONG. . . ."

"Empty!" said the dog.

The second cream can said, "DONG. . . ." too, but the third one when the dog kicked it sounded full: "THOOOK. . . ."

The dog knocked off the lid, lifted the can between his front paws, and guzzled down the whole four gallons.

"Ahhhh!" he said, "That's better. . . ."

And back he sidled — out to the pasture where Davey was still hanging on the barbed wire fence.

"You're mean, dog!" said Davey, "Really mean!"

"I am mean," said the dog, grinning, "It's true."

"Poor Old John!" said Davey, "Well, at least he has the skin off the legs to enjoy."

"He likes the skin off the legs, does he?" said the dog.

"Next to foot bottoms, he likes skin off the legs the best," said Davey, "skin off the legs and a bottle of Pendleton's Pepper Juice to wash it down. . . ."

"Is skin off the legs really salty?" asked the dog. He wanted to be mean, but he didn't know if he could stand any more salty.

"Oh, no," said the boy, "Skin off the legs is more sour than salty."

"Too bad," said the dog. "I like salty. But if sour is all that's available, I'll eat sour."

"I said you were mean before, dog, but I didn't know how mean," said Davey. But he pulled off his jeans and handed them to the dog. There was a lot of rock salt still in the pockets of those jeans.

The dog grabbed the jeans and chewed them down, salt and all. He looked at Davey with a kind of hurt look in his eyes, but he didn't say anything. The inside of his mouth felt like he's just swallowed the whole Sahara Desert.

He sidled off across the pasture at a run. He sidled up to the pump in the middle of Old John Perkins's yard. He stuck his snout under the spout and worked the handle up and down with one hind leg — scree haw! scree haw! scree haw! But the well was dry.

He sidled over to the milk shed and started kicking cream cans, but they all said, "DONG. . . ."

He sidled back out into the yard. He tried to lick his lips, but there was no spit in him. He had just about made up his mind to dry up and die right there when he heard the screen door banging and cast a white eye over at the house. He was that desperate that he didn't hesitate a moment — he sidled over to the house and right in through the back door. He scritched across the linoleum and over to the refrigerator and opened the door.

"Ah ha!" he thought. "Pendleton's Pepper Juice!"

He grabbed the bottle, twisted off the top, put the bottle to his parched lips, and tipped his head back.

"That's better!" he said when the last drop was gone. "Now I'm going go out and eat that boy, and if that makes Old John Perkins mad, I'm glad."

He stepped out the door and . . . that's when the Pepper Juice hit him! He started to sneeze, and he sneezed so hard that he blew himself sideways to Sunday. Old John Perkins found bits of scruffy fur around the place for weeks after that.

Meanwhile, out in the north pasture Davey finally hit on a solution to his problem. He unbuttoned his shirt and squirmed out of it, leaving it hanging on the fence.

He felt a bit silly walking home in his underwear. And he knew he was going to catch heck from his mom.

"Still," he said to himself, "it's better than being inside a sideways-walking dog."

And you really can't argue with that.

Epitaph for a Juggling Poet

Aᴍᴏᴍᴇɴᴛ's ɪɴᴀᴛᴛᴇɴᴛɪᴏɴ ᴀɴᴅ a long weary road brought Gordon Tompkins to New Totem and the coffee shop of the Totem House Hotel. He was sitting there watching appreciatively as Lynnette Trotter came around the end of the counter and headed toward his table carrying a dish of apple pie in one hand and the coffee pot in the other.

"There you go, Lefty," she said. Lynnette was a kidder. If you were fat, she'd call you Slim, if you were short, she'd call you Stretch. Gordon's left arm was missing from just above the elbow. She put the pie down in front of him. "Warm up your coffee?"

She grinned at him and winked, and more than the coffee got warm.

Gordon watched Lynnette walk away, pulled a paper napkin out of the holder and, right then and there, penned this fateful verse:

A Cute Waitress

There was a cute waitress named Lynn
Who brought me my meal with a grin.
When she plunked down the pie
With a wink of her eye
My poor heart went into a spin.

He left the poem on the table when he'd finished, and Lynnette, not being one to think things through all that thoroughly, showed it to her boyfriend. Big John was a brawler and a bully — a handsome man, but mean. He went looking for the one-armed poet, and he found him. The next verse that Gordon Tompkins wrote was penned from his bed at Sisters of Mercy Hospital:

My Nurse
I celebrate now with this verse,
That angel of mercy, my nurse.
She sooth-es my brow,
She brings me my chow,
She smiles when I mutter and curse.

Sister Philomena showed the poem around to all the patients and their visitors and to the other nurses. A few days later, Lynnette came to visit.

"Don't worry, Lefty," she said, "Big John's working out of town for a few weeks. I guess I shouldn't have showed him the poem, but I didn't really think you meant it, and it was a nice poem. Did you know my mom writes poetry, too? That's not what she's most famous for, though. She's most famous for her chocolate fudge. I brought you some."

And Lefty Tompkins, having tasted Ma Trotter's legendary fudge, was moved to write:

The Fudge Poem
Ma Trotter makes fudge smooth and yummy.
It slides down your throat to your tummy.
It tastes quite divine.
Hey! That piece is mine!
Get your own piece, you greedy great dummy!

Ma, being a poet herself, was quick to recognize quality when she saw it. She took the poem down to the offices of the local weekly newspaper, *The New Totem Gusher*, and showed it to Don Murphy, the Arts and Entertainment Editor. Don was keen to run the piece in the next issue, but he didn't know if he should run it on page four in the Food For Thought column (since it was a food item) or on page five in the Names In The News column (since Ma Trotter was a well-known local celebrity). In the end, the Editor-In-Chief, who was also Don Murphy, decided to run the poem as his editorial for the week.

"The editorial page is there for me to express my opinion," he said in justification of his decision, "and that poem expresses, precisely, my opinion of Ma Trotter's chocolate fudge. Besides, it's my paper, and I can print what I like on the editorial page."

Lots of other people must have liked the poem, too, because the paper got half a dozen letters saying could Don please run a poem every week instead of his regular editorial.

And so it was that Lefty Tompkins became something of a Poet Laureate of the Vast Northern Prairie. His poems became the milestones that marked the highway of history on the Vast Northern Prairie. When Sue and Barry White won a trip to Las Vegas, Lefty offered this congratulatory rhyme:

Sour Grapes on not Winning the Trip to Las Vegas Even Though I Bought Twenty Tickets

Sue and Barry got on the bus
And left for Vegas in a cloud of dust.
Now will we crow?
Not us! Oh, no.
When they come back, and they are bust.

When Colonel Sanders came to town to open the Kentucky

Fried Chicken store and rode in the New Totem Days Parade, Lefty wrote a poem to commemorate the event:

On the Occasion of Colonel Sanders' Visit
to New Totem
The Colonel's his name, and he fries-es
Chicken pieces — wings, breast-es and thigh-es.
He never fries toe-es
Or neck-es or noses.
His buckets they come in two sizes.

Lefty liked to eat, and he wrote a lot of poems about food. There was his famous paean to Mark's Cafe:

Mark's Cafe
Let's all go down to Mark's Caf-eh
For a shake, or a Coke and a laugh, eh!
For a burger'n cheese
Fries and gravy? Yes, please!
And all for a buck and a half, hey!

and his poem about Spencer's Bakery and their legendary Sweet Crust Bread. . . .

Spencer's Bakery
Spencer's Bakery is the store
For Sweet Crust Bread and so much more.
Cookies? They got!
Pies? They're fresh hot!
Spencer's Bakery — treats galore!

Lefty spent a lot of time at Spencer's Bakery and, if you ask my opinion, I think he was sort of sweet on Sally. Lefty wrote a lot of his more famous love poems on paper napkins sitting at the counter at Spencer's Bakery drinking coffee and eating doughnuts. This is probably his most famous:

A Lass from the Prairie

There was a young lass from the prairie
Who was light on her feet — like a fairy.
But she danced on my heart
And broke it apart
And waltzed off with my best friend, Larry.

As was fitting for a Poet Laureate, Lefty wrote about all the important things that affected the lives of the people he loved — like the weather. There's a lot of weather in that country and most of it's cold. This is one of Lefty's weather poems:

Bridget

A tender young lady named Bridget
Went out in the weather so fridget.
It was forty below
And starting to snow
And poor little Bridget turned riget.

Dora Ritter and some other ladies made a big quilt for the New Totem Fall Fair a couple of years ago. Each square of the quilt showed a scene from around that area or showed some big event that had happened. I think of Lefty's poems as being kind of like the thread that holds that quilt together. There was one square with a scene of the bridge over the Peaceful River collapsing, and Lefty wrote about that. There was another with a picture of a loaf of Sweet Crust Bread and you already know the poem Lefty wrote about Sweet Crust Bread.

There was a square with a picture of a D9 Cat; there are six or seven poems in Lefty's book about Cats. There was a picture of the big oil derrick in front of the Civic Arena and one of Colonel Sanders standing in front of the new Kentucky Fried Chicken store with Miss Wing and Miss Breast and Miss Thigh. And right in the middle of that quilt — four squares big — there was a picture of Cindy-Lou Pratt! She was one of Lefty's favourite singers and this is a little poem that Lefty dedicated to Cindy-Lou:

When Cindy-Lou Pratt Came to Town
She flew into town with her band.
Their music was quite simply . . . grand.
The songs Cindy belted
I'm sure that they melted
The coldest of hearts in the land.

When Lefty died, Don Murphy ran a piece on him on the front page of the *New Totem Gusher*. LEFTY'S LEFT US was the headline, and it went like this:

Lefty Tompkins has been called the Poet Laureate of the Vast Northern Prairie, and he may well have been — that's for history to decide. I know I liked his poems, and everybody else did, too. We'll miss him on the editorial page.

Lefty wrote about lots of things and people and the weather, but one thing Lefty never did write much about was himself. I thought you might like to know a little about the man.

His real name wasn't Lefty; it was Gordon.

After he was born, Gordon lived back east near Toronto for most of his life. He never planned to be a poet. He started out being a juggler, standing on the street corner and juggling for change. He made a reputation for himself as the Juggling Lumberjack — juggling chainsaws and axes and cork boots. But one day when he was juggling chain saws, he lost his concentration for a split second and cut off his left arm just above the elbow.

After that he gave up juggling and moved from job to job and town to town until he came here and became a poet.

Lefty died the way he lived. He was trying to juggle three bowling balls with one hand and say a poem at the same time when one of the balls came down on his head and cracked his skull.

We all liked Lefty a lot, and we'll miss him. Too bad the bowling ball didn't.

Lefty wrote one last poem the day he died. The undertaker found it in the pocket of Lefty's jeans. It seems like Lefty knew he was running out of rhymes and didn't want to trust his epitaph to any lesser poet. Here is that poem:

Epitaph for a Juggling Poet

Hold onto your nickels and dimes.
This busker has run out of time.
With the turn of each season
He looked for a reason,
But made do, in the end, with a ryhme.

You can get your copy of THE COLLECTED POEMS OF LEFTY TOMPKINS at *The New Totem Gusher* for $7.95.

The New Snow Dance

ON THE WAY HOME FROM Charleen's house, Brandi passed the big field behind the high school where the high school kids played soccer in the Fall and the Spring. Now the field was covered with snow. The sun on the new snow sparkled like a million stars, and the sky was so blue it was music to her eyes.

Brandi stopped and looked at the smooth, crisp sheet of white. In all the whole big field there wasn't a single track; not one footprint — not even a bird's!

Brandi walked over to the edge of the field. She put out one foot and set it down in that expanse of trackless white. She lifted up her foot again and looked . . . the first and only track in that whole white field of snow!

Then . . . across the field she went making all kinds of different tracks.

She swung her feet this way and this and made big wavy tracks.

She pointed her toes out to the sides and made tractor tracks.

She made one-foot hopping tracks.

She made running tracks and tiptoe tracks.

She made twirling tracks.

She made two-feet-together jumping tracks: rabbit tracks.

She shuffled her feet going around this way and around this way until she had shuffled a Valentine in the snow.

She made pigeon-toed tracks.

She made leaping tracks and baby step tracks and giant step tracks.

While Brandi was making tracks, a grey bus pulled up beside the big double doors at the end of the high school gym. Three men and two women got off the bus and headed into the school. But one of the women — the tall one in the black coat — saw Brandi making tracks there in the field and turned and watched. When Brandi make her last track and started for home, the tall woman walked over to the edge of the field and looked at the patterns that Brandi had traced. The woman put her foot in the place where Brandi had made that first track. If Brandi had turned to look she would have been surprised to see a tall woman in a black coat following her tracks — giant step and baby step, leap and twirl — across the snowy field.

Not that afternoon but the next, Brandi's mom said to her, "Lynette went to see those dancers last night — the ones that are dancing in the high school gym. She said we should go. Would you like to go?"

So that evening Honey Dewhurst and Brandi walked in a swirl of snow to the high school gym to see The Saxon Troupe Dancers from Edmonton.

The dancers were beautiful.

They were wild.

They were like butterflies and tigers.

They were silly.

And they were sad.

"What do think, Brandi?" Honey whispered.

"I like it," said Brandi. "Even the sad dances."

"The last dance is just going to start," her mom whispered. "It's a new dance that Anna Saxon just made up. She calls it 'New Snow' . . . shhhh. . . ."

The music started. It sparkled like a million stars. A tall woman wearing a black coat, mittens and ballet slippers ran onto the stage. She stopped. She reached out one foot and placed it carefully down. She lifted her foot, looked where she had stepped and smiled. The music got louder. It made Brandi think of the color blue.

The dancer stepped again, and then, suddenly . . . across the stage she went. . . . She swung her feet this way and this and made big wavy tracks.

She pointed her toes out to the sides and made tractor tracks.

She made one-foot hopping tracks.

She made running tracks and tiptoe tracks.

She made twirling tracks.

She made two-feet-together jumping tracks: rabbit tracks.

She shuffled her feet going around this way and around this way dancing a Valentine.

She made pigeon-toed tracks.

She made leaping tracks and baby step tracks and giant step tracks.

Then, twirling and twirling, she twirled herself into a ball and sat very still. The music stopped.

The audience clapped.

Anna Saxon stood up, brushed the snow off her coat, bowed once and left the stage.

The dancing was finished.

When Brandi and her mom went outside it was still snowing. Honey tucked Brandi's scarf tighter around Brandi's chin. She tucked Brandi's mittens into her sleeves. She pulled Brandi's snow pants down over the tops of her boots. And off they went into the snow-swirling night.

When they were passing the field behind the high school, Brandi saw that the tracks that she had made the day before had all disappeared.

"Look, Mom," she said. "No tracks."

They stopped and watched the snow dusting down.

"Want to make some tracks, Mom?"

"Sure," said her mom. "Let's. . . ."

And so, to the soft yellow music of the street lamp, Brandi Dewhurst and her mom danced a New Snow Dance for Two across the snowy field.

Leaning Into the Wind

Half the time it was a curse, and half the time it was a blessing, and the rest of the time you hardly noticed because it was blowing pretty well every minute and you kind of got used to it. The wind was just a fact of life on the Vast Northern Prairie, blowing out of the southwest day after day — sometimes blowing cold and sometimes hot, sometimes blowing mean and sometimes blowing sweet, but always blowing.

It could be a curse if you were Andy Trotter and you'd just started junior high and now you had to walk kitty corner all the way across town facing into the wind. On a nice fall day you could figure leaving the house a half hour early to account for the wind slowing you down. On a cold winter day, with snow or ice mixed in with the wind, you had to add in an hour at least. You were going to have to walk backward most of the way, because your face would freeze if you walked facing the wind for more than a minute or two. And then you were going to want to stop at the King Koin Laundromat on the way so you could warm up your coat and mitts. A dime would give you ten minutes of hot tumble dry, and you'd feel almost warm the rest of the way to school.

But coming home in the afternoon would be great. With the wind behind you, you could be home in time to watch *The Rifleman* before supper.

The wind was a curse if you were driving to Hunter's Bridge, because most of the way you'd be heading into the wind, and you'd burn three or four times as much gas as usual. Coming back to New Totem, though, you didn't even have to turn on the engine. You could just shift into neutral and let the wind push you along the valley and up that windy hill above Deer Meadows. Going to Bear Canyon was just the opposite — cheap to get there, expensive to get back.

Actually, the wind was ALWAYS a factor to take into account when you were driving in that country, even if you were driving side-on to the wind. It'd soon get to be second nature to steer a bit to the left all the time you were heading northwest to adjust for the wind trying to push to toward the right. And, of course, you'd have to steer a bit to the right when you were travelling southeast. After a while it got to be second nature. When the wind stopped blowing all of a sudden, though, THAT could be a problem. Say you were heading toward Tailor's Flats and steering a little to the right like you should. And then you see a flatbed truck with a load of hay bales stopped on the shoulder up ahead, and you start wondering if the driver's stopped because he's got engine trouble or if he's just out there watering the stubble. You come up on the east of the truck. The hay bales are blocking the wind on that side, though, and because you're wondering instead of thinking, you keep on steering to the right and in a wink you find yourself parked up against the truck with hay bales for a hood ornament. That's the kind of thing that could happen if you were driving in the wind and not paying attention.

Walking was the same thing. Nobody in New Totem ever stood up completely straight when they were outside. They were always leaning a bit in one direction or the other depending on which way the wind was blowing. And because of that, people fell down a lot.

You'd come out of Totem Gifts, get leaned at just the right angle, and then you'd turn the corner by the IGA and if you didn't adjust your lean fast enough — bang! — you'd be down.

The sound of the wind blowing — it was a sound to make you curse or a sound to make you glad, depending on which way you were going. But for Will and Wilf Turner the sound of the wind was the sound of paper money riffling under your thumb. As long as the wind kept blowing, Will and Wilf kept making money.

Will and Wilf's father, Wilt Turner had started the business when he first came to New Totem back in the forties. He noticed how a lot of the buildings in town were leaning over toward the northeast, because of the wind blowing on them all the time from the southwest. After a house got leaning so far that you couldn't keep knick-knacks hanging on the southwest wall, people would just rip it down and build a new one. Well, that was an expensive business, and Wilt thought he could fix the leaning problem cheaper and faster. He bought a couple of hydraulic jacks and a half dozen 12 X 12 timbers and set himself up in business as W. Turner and Sons Building Rotators. (Wilf didn't have any sons at the time, but he had foresight.)

For a third of what it would cost you to tear down a leaning building and rebuild it straight again, Wilt would come, jack your place up, turn it 180 degrees and set it back on the foundation. Of course, if you had indoor plumbing and gas lines to contend with that cost extra. But Wilt alway turned people's outhouses for free as a customer service.

Besides being cheaper, Wilt's service had longer lasting results. Once your leaning building was turned 180 degrees, it was actually leaning INTO the wind. In the time it would take a rebuilt to start leaning toward the northeast, your Turner-rotated building would just be blowing upright, and you could still count on a few more years before it would be leaning enough that you had to rotate it again.

Will and Wilf helped out with the business from the time they were really small. A lot of people in New Totem at that time didn't bother with a basement under the house, and sometimes the crawl space was pretty cramped for a man Wilt's size. So Wilt'd once in a while bring along the boys and send them under the house with a hydraulic jack each, and he'd keep watch with a flashlight and make sure they got the jacks positioned right. Then once they'd lifted the building a foot or so, Wilt'd climb under and finish the job himself.

When the boys were eighteen and sixteen, Wilt was killed in a tragic accident. He was rotating a big three-holer that belonged to the then mayor, Del Tailor, when a big gust of wind came up and toppled the outhouse right on top of him. Will and Wilf changed the name of the company to Turner Bros. Building Rotators and finished the job the next day.

Despite the fact that it had taken their dad, the Turner brothers never thought ill of the wind. For them, it was a blessing as long as it blew. It kept them fed and provided for their families . . . . until the hydro company built the dam.

Life's a funny thing. You'd think if there was one thing you could depend on it would be a wind out of the southwest, but, no, it seems even the wind'll change when you're not watching. When they built the dam and flooded the river valley west of Hunter's Bridge, the wind seemed to get confused. It was always used to sweeping down the east slope of the mountains and straight on across the prairie. And now, all of a sudden, there was this huge lake there at the foot of the mountains. By the time the wind had skittered around on the water for a while it was all twisted up so it didn't know if it was a gust or a gale. When it came off the lake it could be blowing any which way.

The wind still blew, of course, but you could never be sure from where to where. It still blew MOSTLY out of the southwest, but often enough it would be blowing in the complete opposite direction. With the wind blowing this way one day and that way the next, the leaning problem kind of took care of itself in most cases and business started to drop off for Turner Bros. House Rotators.

About the same time, too, New Totem got a building inspector and people seemed to be getting a lot more particular about how many nails they used when they built something.

Between the lake and the nails, the building rotating business was pretty much a thing of the past in New Totem by the time Will's boy, Wilkie, was old enough to take an interest in the business (not that he did, in any case). And Wilf's girl, Willa, married a dentist from Calgary, so she didn't have much use for a couple hydraulic jacks and a bunch of 12 X 12 timbers. One day in June, the Turner brothers, Will and Wilf, nailed a 2 X 4 across the door of the garage where they kept the jacks and the timbers, got in the motor home with their wives, Bonnie and Sherry, and left New Totem for good.

Last I heard of Will and Bonnie they were living in Salmon Arm. The wind doesn't blow there much, but Will and Bonnie feel right at home. The place is so hilly you've always got to be leaning in one direction or another just to keep from falling over.

I heard a strange story about Wilf, and I don't know if I should believe it or not. Sherry passed away a couple of years ago, and Wilf disappeared a while later. Maurice King — I'm not asking you to believe this; I'm just passing it on — Maurice said that a month or so after Sherry's funeral, he was out in the town ambulance rounding up stray dogs when he saw Wilf. Wilf was climbing up the oil derrick in front of the Civic Arena. And when he got to the top, Maurice says, Wilf opened his coat and held it out like a pair of wings. A big gust of wind came along right then, and Wilf sort of leaned into it. The wind lifted Wilf off the top of the derrick and carried him away toward the northeast. Maurice said he watched, and Wilf just kept rising up higher and higher until he was just a tiny speck in the sky. And then he was gone.

The Ghost in the Garbage Can

LAST YEAR THERE WAS a blizzard on Hallowe'en and a minus-ninety-degree wind chill factor. The year before that, Hallowe'en fell on a school night. But this year, everything looked perfect. This year Fudgie Trotter, his brother Patrick, Fudgie's best friend, Kurt Gerber, and his other best friend, Dougie Bowman would — for sure! — make it into the *Guinness Book of World Records* for collecting the most candy ever collected in a single Hallowe'en night.

It was three o'clock on Saturday afternoon, October 31st. Fudgie, his brother and his two best friends where sitting in the Trotter's living room conducting a last minute review of the plan. All four of them were dressed as ghosts. Most kids in New Totem that night would be dressed as either ghosts or clowns. There was no room under a Superman costume or a pixie outfit for a heavy winter coat, and if you were going for maximum candy it was more important to be warm than original.

"Patrick," said Fudgie, his voice somewhat muffled by the sheet that was pulled tight over his head and secured with a few wraps of gauze bandage around his neck, "What is your mission?"

"I ride my bike to Emerson's Junk Yard and lock it up in a safe place. I go to all the trailers in the trailer court, and then I go to those three apartment buildings by the Tasty Freeze. Then I go up one street and down the other on all the streets between 100th Street and the edge of town, and go to every single house. . . ."

"Where do we rendezvous?"

"At the corner where the Co-op Store is," said Patrick, "and I gotta be there before the siren goes."

"That's good," said Fudgie.

That last item was important. In New Totem, the fire siren sounded for about thirty seconds every evening exactly at nine o'clock. No kids were allowed to be out on the street after that. Fudgie knew of at least one kid who swore he was dragged home in handcuffs when the police caught him out after the siren. Rumours circulated concerning windowless cells in dark warrens under the police station, and there were whispers of thumb screws and chains. But the Mounties would be the least of a kid's worries if he was out after the siren on Hallowe'en Night — after the siren on Hallowe'en Night the high school kids came out. They went around tipping over toilets and soaping up windows and wrapping the teachers' houses in toilet paper. And worst of all, after the siren they could steal any little kid's candy with impunity. If you were out after the siren and high school kids stole your candy, nobody cared. If you told your parents, they just said, "Serves you right for being out after the siren. We told you." And no kid in his right mind was going to go to the police and complain.

"That's good you remembered about the siren," said Fudgie.

"And Dad will be there to pick us up in the pick-up truck, and he'll load up all the bikes and take us back to our house," Patrick recited.

"That's right!" said Fudgie, "But what about if you get hungry?"

"If I get hungry and I absolutely have to eat something, I have to mark it down in my notebook." Patrick rummaged around under his sheet for a while and finally extended a hand holding a small coil-bound notebook, "Except I don't have to mark down peanuts or apples because they don't count."

"Good! You got your extra pillow case?"

Patrick nodded.

"You other guys ready?"

Kurt Gerber nodded. He would be responsible for canvassing the southeast quadrant of the town. Dougie Bowman nodded. Dougie would take the northwest. Fudgie himself would be responsible for hitting every inhabited house and apartment in the most densely populated northeast quarter of the town. He was carrying TWO extra pillow cases.

A few minutes later, the four boys were on their bicycles dispersing toward the four outermost corners of the town of New Totem. Fudgie figured that four o'clock was about the earliest that they could decently start knocking on doors, and he wanted them all in place and ready to go by then.

By five o'clock, Fudgie had finished all the houses north and east of Abalard Elementary School, and he had over a quarter of a sack full. He stopped in the school playground to rest on one of the swings and eat a few peanuts and a Wagon Wheel. He marked the Wagon Wheel down in his notebook and headed off again on what promised to be the most difficult portion of his journey.

Black Gold Petroleums had at some point in history built a subdivision in the northeast corner of town to provide subsidized housing for oil company employees. Black Pete, as the area was called, was the only area of town that wasn't laid out in nice tidy rectangles. Paper boys had been known to venture into the convoluted crescents and snaking roads of Black Pete, never to return.

"The houses are nice and close together anyway," Fudgie told himself as he plunged into the maze.

He had budgetted an hour to cover all the houses in Black Pete, but it was nearly 7:30 before he found himself back on 105th Avenue again. He had gotten locked in on White Mud Crescent and had gone around three times before he realized that one jack-o-lantern was starting to look very familiar. He could very well have done the same thing on several other crescents; there was no way to know now. But he did know that he was an hour behind schedule with a lot of houses between him and 100th Street.

And his bag — three quarters full now — was slowing him down. Well, he'd just have to do what he could do.

He'd filled up one bag and was well started on the second when he got to the Northern Twilight Seniors Apartments near the Legion. It was 8:15.

There were about twenty apartments in the building and at every single apartment Fudgie was forced to sing a song or dance a little dance before the little lady behind the door would fork over the candy. Looking back later, Fudgie realized that he'd had to do a lot of work for very little return at the Northern Twilight Seniors Apartments. And worse than that — by the time he came out the front door again, there were only four minutes left before the nine o'clock siren sounded.

Fudgie judged that he could make it the rest of the way with a minute to spare, but as he was hurrying down the front steps of the apartment building, the exhausted fabric of his bulging pillow case gave up the struggle. Strand parted from strand with a tired sigh, and Fudgie's world record candy hoard flowed out onto the ground.

He took out his third pillow case. With his breath coming in panicky little sobs, he scooped candy and rocks and dead grass into the bag. He leaped to his feet and went running — as fast as a fat little ghost with fifty pounds of candy can run — down the street toward the corner. But just as he reached Volger's Glass, the air was filled with a dreadful wailing sound — the nine o'clock siren! He was too late. Even if his dad hung around and waited at the corner, there were still four more blocks to go before he got there.

Up ahead, on the other side of 100th Street, a door opened and a gang of high school kids came down the walk. Fudgie ducked into the space between Volger's Glass and the second-hand store. He could hear teenage voices getting louder as the gang came down the street.

Fudgie's first thought was for the candy. He had to hide the candy! He looked around, his eyes wild in the dark rings of his ghost mask. Where? Where? There were a couple of old garbage cans up against the wall, and a pile of sheets of cardboard, and .. . yes . . . that would be perfect! . . . a wooden packing crate filled with shredded newspaper. Fudgie clawed out a hollow space in the shredded newspaper and dropped his two bags of candy into the nest that he had made. He covered his treasure with paper and put the top on the crate.

He crept out to the corner of the second-hand store and peeked carefully around. There were three of them — standing on the corner with Coke bottles gleaming in their hands, the fire from their cigarettes glowing like demon eyes and their hair goop glinting in the cold light of the street lamp — high school kids! Suddenly, one of them turned and looked straight at Fudgie and waved. Fudgie yanked his head back. Fudgie's brain started yelling at Fudgie's feet to run, but before his feet could get organized, Fudgie heard voices approaching from the other direction. The high school kid had been waving at some other high school kids who were coming down the street the other way. That meant he probably hadn't seen Fudgie at all; but it also meant that Fudgie was surrounded.

Fudgie was a fast thinker. In the time it took to breath twice, half a dozen scenarios played themselves out in his mind. He'd bluff his way out . . . pretend to BE a high school kid . . . stupid idea . . . He'd cry and show them the ripped pillow case and tell them how he'd lost all his candy, and they'd let him go . . . Ha! He'd run for it! They'd never catch him! They'd catch him. They caught him every time. On the third breath, he imagined himself hunkered down in one of those old garbage cans. He saw the high school kids pass by. He saw himself getting out of the garbage can and . . . and . . . he'd have to worry about that later. He darted across to the garbage cans and lifted off the lid of the one furthest from the street. It was full. He lifted off the lid of the other one. Empty! In the wink of a witch's eye, the garbage can was full of Fudgie Trotter, and the lid was on.

The voices faded away after a while, but Fudgie waited a bit longer to be sure. Slowly, he lifted the lid. No high school kids in sight. He was climbing out of the garbage can, when he noticed something that he hadn't noticed before — the bottom was all rusted out of the can.

Fudgie's brain kicked in again. He saw a garbage can with little feet scurrying across town in the dark. Every time a high school kid appeared, the garbage can set itself down on the curb and looked innocent. When the high school kid had gone by, the garbage can picked itself up and scurried on again.

There was nothing to hang onto on the inside of the can to lift it up with, but with a bit of squirming around, Fudgie found he could push out with his elbows and hold the can from slipping down while he straightened up his legs. And there was a little hole where one of handles had come off that he could look out through. This was a good plan. He got stood up and started scurrying toward the street, except that it was more of a scuffle than a scurry. He could only move his feet a baby step forward each time. But he'd get there eventually.

He stopped to reconnoitre when he got to the sidewalk. He scrunched back down and lifted the lid so he could see if there was anything coming. Nothing coming. He stood up and pointed himself back in the direction of the old folks' home. He hadn't covered much distance when his arms started to ache and he had to scrunch down to rest. He'd no sooner got settle when he heard an eerie whistling sound approaching. Fudgie squinted out through his spy hole. It was a high school kid — a loner — coming down the street toward him. He was whistling a horrible tuneless whistle that stopped suddenly when the high school kid was about six feet away. Fudgie saw him put his Coke bottle to his lips and guzzle down the last of his Coke. Then to Fudgie's horror, the high school kid walked straight toward him. Fudgie heard the lid rattle as the high school kid grabbed the handle. Fudgie clamped his eyes shut and strangled the scream that was trying to force its way up from his belly. The lid lifted, Fudgie felt a dull thump on top of his head, the lid clattered again, and all was still. The tuneless whistling melted away into the night.

It wasn't until that moment that Fudgie remembered his hoard of candy. The thought of shuffling back to get it made Fudgie moan aloud.

"I can't do it!" he thought. "Besides, there isn't room in here for me and two pillow cases full of candy. When I get home, Dad will drive me back to pick it up."

Cheered by that thought, Fudgie struggled to his feet and went shuffling on along the dark street. He wondered if there was a *Guinness Book of World Records* record for longest distance walked inside a garbage can. He started counting shuffles with one part of his brain while another part tried to estimate how long each shuffle was and tried to work out how many shuffles there would be to a mile. In another part of his brain he was standing in front of the class showing off his picture in the *Guinness Book of World Records*, and Mrs. Bowes was smiling.

Suddenly, all the parts of Fudgie's brain stopped what they were doing and wondered why everything was so bright. Then a voice spoke — a menacing mechanical voice — and all parts of Fudgie's brain knew he was in big trouble: "You there, garbage can! Stay right where you are. This is the police! We've got you surrounded!"

Fudgie stopped.

Except for the radio squawking and the different smell, the ride home in the police car wasn't that much different from riding home in Kurt's dad's car. But if Fudgie was disappointed, he didn't say so.

The young Mountie told him how his parents had got worried about him and had phoned the police station to ask them to keep an eye out for a lost ghost.

"You just about had me fooled with the garbage can disguise," he told Fudgie, "but disguises was my best subject at Mountie school."

Fudgie smiled a humble little smile and thought to himself, "This guy is pretty friendly. I wonder what he'd say if I asked him if he'd mind taking me back to get my candy?" But, of course, he didn't ask and a couple minutes later, they were home.

Fudgie sat at the kitchen table listening to his mom talking to the Mountie. His dad was out in the pick-up driving around town trying to find him. Then the door closed, and his mom came into the kitchen.

"Andrew Trotter!" she said. "Where have you been? Didn't you hear the siren? Don't you know what that siren means? Do you know how worried I've been? Do you think I like having my boy dragged home by the police like a criminal? Well, do you?"

"No. . . ." said Fudgie.

Ma plunked herself down and picked up the teapot.

"Well, I'm glad you're okay," She shook her head ruefully and poured herself another cup of tea. "Get out of that costume and get to bed now."

Fudgie thought it might not be a good idea to ask if maybe his dad could drive him back down to get the bags of candy.

On the way downtown the next morning, Kurt and Dougie heard the story of Fudgie's adventures. Patrick had already heard them in the whispered dark of their bedroom the night before.

"You better have a lot of candy if we're going to make a World Record, Fudgie," said Dougie. He was pulling his little brother's wagon to carry home Fudgie's hoard. "Your little brother ate most of his candy before he even got home, and he didn't mark one single thing down in his notebook."

"Yeah, well you only got about six things!" retorted Patrick.

"Hey! How would you like to get chased by a Doberman pincher with hydrophobia?"

"Ha! How do you know he had hydrophobia?"

"He was foaming at the mouth, that's how! Don't you know anything?"

Dougie had had to give up after only ten houses because of a rabid Doberman pinscher. And Kurt had stepped into a ditch and had gotten icy water in his boot, so he had to go home early, too.

"Well, I got lots!" declared Fudgie, "Probably enough for a World Record all by myself. It's in a wooden box beside the glass store."

But it wasn't. The space between Volger's Glass and the second-hand store was empty. The garbage can was gone. The pile of cardboard was gone. And the wooden crate was gone.

"It's gone!" cried Fudgie, "The box is gone! My candy . . . is gone. . . ."

"Are you sure this is the right place?" said Dougie.

"YES!" Fudgie yelled angrily. He looked like he wanted to kick something, so Patrick moved a ways away. "YES! There was a box here. It was made out of sort of wooden slats and it was full of chopped up newspaper! It was HERE!"

"Well, it's not here now," said Kurt, "I guess that's that."

It wasn't quite, though.

When Ma heard what had happened, she felt so sad that she made Fudgie and Patrick a whole batch of chocolate fudge, and they got to stay up and eat fudge and watch *Bonanza* even though there was school the next day.

Then, the following Wednesday afternoon, Fudgie and Patrick were having a plate of fries and gravy at Mark's Cafe while their mom was shopping at the Co-op. They'd just got their fries when four high school kids came in and sat in one of the booths. One of the high school kids dug into the pockets of his jacket with both hands and came out with both fists full of candy. He dumped the candy in a pile on the table.

"Two big bags full!" he said. "I was helping my dad haul away some garbage from behind the store and there they were in this box — two big bags full of candy!"

Fudgie looked at Patrick. Patrick looked at Fudgie. Fudgie picked up a French fry and stirred it around in the ketchup. Patrick squared his shoulders and pushed his plate away. He jumped down from his stool.

"Sit down, Patrick!" Fudgie barked.

Mark looked over from where he was standing by the cash register. The high school kids looked over, too. Patrick stood for a moment glaring at the high school kids, and then he looked again at Fudgie, shrugged his shoulders and sat back down.

"Eat your fries," said Fudgie. He ate his, but they didn't taste as good as usual somehow.

The Fortune Cookie God Speaks

Y OU DON'T GET TO HAVE a reputation for culinary craftsmanship like Ma Trotter had by burning things. Ma NEVER burned anything she cooked — not even marshmallows over a campfire. While everyone else was dancing in the twilight, madly wagging willows sticks aflame with blistering gobs of sugar, Ma would be patiently turning her marshmallow round and round, holding it exactly the right distance from a glowing coal, watching it turn a heartwarming golden brown. Ma took great pride in never burning a marshmallow or anything else she ever cooked. Fudgie knew that, and so it was with deep gratitude that he watched his mother fling the smoking remains of the stew out the window.

Patrick, hearing the clamber and smelling the choking fumes, came rushing in from the living room where he'd been watching *Razzle Dazzle* on TV. He came through the door just in time to see the tail of the stew comet catch on the breeze and go wafting toward the alley. In a couple of minutes, the acrid smell of it would invade Mr. and Mrs. Webster's prim, needlepoint-appointed living room and re-ignite the smouldering coals of the neighbourhood conflagration that had started when Patrick had recruited the Webster's geriatric poodle to play the role of a lion to his Tarzan.

"What happened to my stew!" cried Patrick.

"I'm sorry, Patrick," said Ma, "I got caught up in my book. . . ." She gestured toward a volume of *Reader's Digest Condensed Stories* lying open on the table, " . . . and I forgot to watch the stew!"

Fudgie glanced out the window and saw Brian Webster coming across his back yard, his long stork legs moving fast.

"Ma," said Fudgie, jerking his head toward the window, "since we can't eat Patrick's stew, how about we go down to the Red Dragon for egg foo-yung."

"Good idea!" said Ma, grabbing her purse from under the chair.

In a wink, they were out the front door, avoiding in one maneuver, more awkward questions about the stew and a confrontation with the offended neighbour.

Fudgie munched on his fortune cookie and re-read the faded red message on the little ribbon of paper: *"DON'T TEMPT FATE."*

"Sorry," he said, silently addressing the Fortune Cookie God. The Fortune Cookie God must have been watching Fudgie pretty closely. The message obviously referred to the stew fiasco. "I won't do it ever again. . . ."

What the Fortune Cookie God was really saying was, "Be real careful what you say to your brother, Fudgie. Don't go putting ideas into his head."

Fudgie had heard that piece of good advice before.

Like the time Fudgie'd said to Patrick who was four and a half at the time, "Patrick, take the car and drive into Big Prairie, and buy me a Superman Comic, okay."

When Patrick went over to the hotel and asked Mr. Bowen, the manager to please go into the beer parlour and ask his dad for the car keys, Mr. Bowen just assumed that Ma had sent the boy.

Patrick's dad, Marvin Trotter, who was just about to launch into a recitation of "The Shooting Of Dan McGrew" when Bowen came to the table, fished in his pocket and handed the keys over without giving it a second thought.

With the car keys clutched in his hand, Patrick stopped at Kenny Wiseman's house.

"Kenny," he said, "I have to drive to Big Prairie to buy a Superman Comic for Fudgie. I need you to come and push the pedals for me."

Patrick knew that the "D" on the shift column meant "Drive" and that "R" meant "go backwards" and, knowing that, he figured he knew enough. But he was too short to steer and push the pedals at the same time.

"When I say 'GO!' you push that one, Kenny," he told his friend, "and when I say 'STOP!' you press that one. I think. . . ."

With Patrick steering and Kenny Wiseman sitting on the floor pushing the pedals, the boys got as far as the Turner's driveway before Patrick, swerving to avoid the Turner's black dog, drove Marvin's big old Mercury Monarch into a ditch full of green water and cattails.

Or the time Fudgie and Patrick were exploring in the Wringle's toolshed and Fudgie, noticing the part-full cans of paint along the shelf over the workbench had commented, "I wonder if Mr. Wringle's going to use this paint? Dad said if we had a bit of extra cash it would be nice to paint the outside of the trailer. . . ."

Or the time Fudgie had mused aloud in Patrick's hearing about how cute Honey's baby would look with a Mohawk haircut. She did too, but that didn't stop Honey from getting mad and cuffing Fudgie and saying, "Be real careful what you say to your brother, Fudgie. Don't go putting ideas into his head!"

The most recent incident had arisen out of Patrick's current fascination with weapons. His arsenal included a blow gun made out of a length of copper tubing (Patrick had been spending a lot of time lately in the kitchen, mixing various herbs and spices in vinegar, beer and/or KoolAid, trying to concoct a lethal poison to put on the tips of his blow gun darts.); a sling shot; a boomerang that wouldn't come back (But which was very effective nonetheless as witnessed by the broken pane of glass in the bathroom window . . .); a rubber-band powered rifle; and a set of bolas made out of a length of clothesline, two old baseballs, and enough black electrician's tape to stretch to Edmonton and back. His newest and best weapon, though, was a long bow made out of a hockey stick.

Since Marvin didn't own a table saw, Patrick had been forced to make a deal with Ma's cousin, Gerald Mackie, who was a carpenter and had a shop behind his house next to Anna's Drive-In. Patrick spent a couple of hours one morning washing Gerald's truck, and, in return, Gerald used his table saw to split the hockey stick lengthwise leaving a section about eight inches long in the centre uncut.

Patrick tied a piece of heavy-duty fishing line to one end of the stick, wrestled the now-pliant wood into a shallow bow shape, and tied it in place with the other end of the fishing line. With his jackknife he carved the uncut section into a hand grip. He scrounged a couple of lengths of quarter-inch dowelling at the lumber yard, attached one-inch finishing nails to the points with electrician's tape, glued on feathers made out of thin cardboard from a cornflakes box, and carved notches in the ends. When he was done, he had a formidable weapon.

"Don't you dare point that thing at any of the other kids!" warned Ma.

"It's a hunting bow, Mom!" said Patrick, "Of course, I wouldn't point it at a human person! Sheesh!"

"A hunting bow?" said Fudgie, "Ha! What are you going to kill? Tigers?"

"If one comes around killing the cows, I might," said Patrick, These were imaginary cows that Patrick was talking about. "But I don't kill things just for fun. I kill to survive. I mostly only kill what I can eat."

"Hey, Great White Hunter," said Fudgie, "Could you go out and shoot me a hamburger deluxe with fries?"

"No," said Patrick, "but I could shoot a moose or a deer. If I shoot a moose or a deer, would you cook it, Mom?"

"Maybe you should start with something small," said Ma with a little grin.

"Yeah," put in Fudgie, "how about shooting a couple of rabbits, and Mom could make a stew."

Several hours later, Patrick walked into the kitchen and flopped the long, stringy, wet-and-glistening, fresh-skinned carcass of a rabbit onto the table.

"There's supper, Mom!" he declared proudly.

Ma gaped at the dead thing on the table.

"Uh . . . Uh . . . " she said, "Uh . . . It's pretty small to feed three, Patrick."

"That's okay," said Patrick, "I got a crow and a squirrel, too."

He went into the utility room and came back with the little flayed bodies dangling from one hand and an onion in the other.

"I was going to save these," he said, "but we can mix them together."

"I don't know. . . . " Ma started to say.

Patrick gave her a hard look and set the onion on the table.

Now, probably the two most famous things that Ma Trotter ever said were:

"The secret of good fudge is in the whipping around."

and

"Give me any three ingredients and an onion and I will make you a stew."

The message in the onion was clear.

When Fudgie came home, Ma was stirring something in a black cast iron pot on the stove.

"What's for supper, Mom?"

"Stew," said Ma, "Rabbit, crow, and squirrel stew. You think I should make some dumplings to go with it?"

"Huh?" said Fudgie, "What kind of stew?"

"Patrick went hunting," said Ma.

At that time the Trotter's house was right on the edge of town. To the east was an empty field, then a big patch of bush, and then a farmer's field beyond that. There weren't any tigers in that patch of bush, or even moose or deer, but there were rabbits and squirrels and crows.

"Mom!" protested Fudgie, "we can't eat that. How do we know Patrick even killed them. They probably died of some kind of horrible disease and he found them and dragged them home. What's that floating in there, Mom? Are those crow's feet floating in there?"

"No, dear," said his mom in a tired voice, "I cut the feet off the crow. Now I promised. . . ."

"Mom! Those animals might have been run over and left on the road. Did you check for tire marks? Did you see the animals with the skins on? Maybe that rabbit was the Webster's cat. Ah, please, Mom, we can't eat that stuff!"

Ma stopped stirring the stew. She looked at Fudgie. She looked toward the living room door and saw Howie the Turtle on the TV wearing a trumpet on his head for a hat. A tear came into her eye as she looked back toward the cast iron pot on the stove.

With a sigh, she turned away from the stove and sat down at the end of the table. She picked up her *Reader's Digest* book, and she said, "Fudgie, could you turn up the heat under that stew a bit? It's not bubbling quite fast enough . . . ."

The Trotter Family Cookbook

THE FOLLOWING ARE selected recipes from the *THE TROTTER FAMILY COOKBOOK*, a Vast Northern Prairie classic featuring all those dishes that made Ma and Honey famous as well as contributions from Lynnette, Fudgie, Patrick, and the rest of the Trotter clan. It is available at the *New Totem Gusher* for $7.95.

CHICKEN IN A NEST
contributed by Patrick Trotter

Ingredients:
a roll of baloney
eggs
seasonings

1. Cut a slice of baloney off the roll. Try to get it as even as you can. Don't make it too thick, but don't get holes in it.
2. Take off the plastic wrapper, but leave the rind on. THIS IS IMPORTANT.
3. Put the slice of baloney in a frying pan over medium heat.
4. When the rind shrinks and the middle of the baloney poinks up, flip it over.

5. Crack an egg into the hollow in the middle of the baloney.
6. Season with salt, pepper, paprika, cayenne pepper and HP Sauce to taste.
7. Sprinkle a few drops of water into the pan and cover the baloney with a pot lid. Cook until the egg stops jiggling.

FRIED BREAD
contributed by Fudgie Trotter

Ingredients:
sliced white bread
butter or margarine
strawberry jam

1. Spread butter or margarine on the bread.
2. Fry it in a frying pan until it is a rich golden brown and the bread is starting to get stiff.
3. Spread on the strawberry jam.

RECIPE FOR A PEACEFUL SUPPER
contributed by Honey Dewhurst

Ingredients:
any really easy recipe from this book
a good book to read

1. Put the food on the table.
2. Say, "Help yourself. There's plenty more on the stove." Help yourself.
3. Hold your book in your left hand.
4. Eat with your right hand.
5. Say,"You kids stop fighting!" when you get to the bottom of the odd-numbered pages. Say, "Yes, dear." when you get to the bottom of the even- numbered pages.
6. DO NOT RESPOND TO DIRECT QUESTIONS OR ALLOW YOURSELF TO BE DRAWN INTO CONVERSATION.

NO-FAIL SANDWICH IDEAS
contributed by Lynnette Trotter

SUGAR SANDWICH: Spread white bread with butter or margarine. Sprinkle on lots of white sugar. Dump off the excess. Serve openfaced.

MUSTARD SANDWICH: Spread white bread with margarine or butter. Add a thin layer of prepared mustard — NOT THE FANCY KIND. Serve openfaced for watching TV. Serve folded or with another piece of bread on top for school lunches or for company.

KETCHUP SANDWICH: Substitute ketchup for mustard in the recipe above. WARNING: don't use too much ketchup if you are going to put this sandwich in your kid's lunch; the ketchup makes the bread all soggy.

SPAGHETTI SAUCE SANDWICH: Get someone else to make some spaghetti sauce (see MA'S EXTRA THICK AND HEARTY BET YOU CAN'T GUESS WHAT'S IN IT SPAGHETTI SAUCE on page 88.) Chill left-over sauce in the refrigerator overnight. Spread sauce on buttered white bread. Put a top on. See WARNING above, but only more so.

BEAN SOUP SANDWICH: Get someone else to make a pot of bean soup. (See BEAN AND HAM SOUP on page 211.) Chill the left-overs in the fridge overnight. The soup should be REALLY thick. Put a glob of beans in a bowl and mash them up with a fork. Spread mashed beans on buttered white bread. Sprinkle with salt and pepper to taste. Put a top on. Eat immediately. WARNING: do not wear anything that needs dry cleaning while eating this sandwich. WARNING: not suitable for school lunches.

PEANUT BUTTER AND DILL PICKLE SANDWICH: Spread white bread with smooth peanut butter. Add sliced dill pickles and a top. For variety try substituting sweet pickles, gerkins, mustard pickles, pickled onions or pickled herring for the dill pickles.

FANCY SANDWICHES: Cut the crust off slices of white bread. Spread slices with peanut butter. Wrap around WHOLE dill pickles. Cut into slices.

A GOOD FOOD JOKE
contributed by Patrick Trotter

This is a good trick to do if your mom is having a bunch of ladies over for tea or if your parents are having a party.

Put two tablespoons full of Eno's Fruit Salts on top of the sugar in the sugar bowl. When one of the ladies puts "sugar" in her tea it will foam up and run over the top of the cup.

DOUGH GODS
contributed by Ma Trotter

Ingredients:
raw bread dough (See WHITE BREAD on page 351)
deep frying fat
an assortment of toppings

1. After you have punched down the bread and before you put it in pans, rip off several hunks (about half the size you would use to make a dinner bun).
2. Stretch and pull each hunk of dough into stringy shapes.
3. Drop into hot fat.
4. Fry dough until golden brown on one side, flip it over and cook the other side.
5. Drain on brown paper.
6. Serve HOT with butter and maple syrup, jam or brown sugar.

MA'S DIET HINTS
contributed by Ma Trotter

If you are feeling hungry between meals, eat black licorice or jujubes. Black licorice is flavored mostly with salt so it doesn't have many calories. If you can only get red licorice, buy stale stuff; you will burn off the extra calories chewing. Jujubes are a good snack because the gelatin in them swells up in your stomach and makes you feel full.

MARVIN'S FAVOURITE OMELETTE
contributed by Ma Trotter

Ingredients:
three eggs
grated mild cheddar cheese or cubed Velveeta Cheese
strawberry jam

1. Beat the eggs in a bowl and pour into a hot frying pan.
2. When the the eggs are starting to set up, add the cheese and two tablespoonfuls (or to taste) of strawberry jam.
3. Fold over and cook a bit more.

QUICK TV SNACK
contributed by Fudgie Trotter

Ingredients:
a jar of Cheez Whiz
a box of Ritz Crackers

1. Spoon Cheez Whiz into one bowl. Put Ritz Crackers in another bowl.
2. Scoop up Cheez Whiz with crackers and eat.

HONEY'S QUICK CUTLETS
contributed by Honey Dewhurst

Ingredients:
a can of canned luncheon meat (Spork, Spam, Vroom, Zoom, Klik or Klam)
egg
milk
flour
fine bread crumbs

1. Slice luncheon meat.
2. Mix egg and milk together.
3. Roll slices of luncheon meat in flour, dip in egg mixture, shake off excess egg mixture, and roll in bread crumbs.
4. Fry in butter until golden brown on both sides.

ARNIE'S FAVOURITE SANDWICH
contributed by Honey Dewhurst

Ingredients:
white bread
orange slices
sliced red or white (not green) onions
butter or margarine

1. Spread slices of bread with butter. HINT: spread the butter extra thick on the slice of bread that is going to be next to the orange slices to keep the juice from sogging into the bread.
2. Layer on orange and onion slices and salt and pepper to taste.
3. Top with a second slice of buttered bread.

DRAGON MILK
contributed by Brandi Dewhurst

Ingredients:
milk
sugar
vanilla

1. Pour the milk.
2. Put in some sugar.
3. Put in vanilla until it gets to be a sort of brownish colour.
4. Mix it with a spoon.

EGG AND DILL PICKLE SANDWICH
contributed by Honey Dewhurst

Ingredients:
white bread
butter or margarine
egg
sliced dill pickles

1. Spread butter or margarine on bread.
2. Fry the egg, breaking the yolk so it will cook hard.
3. Put cooked egg and pickle slices on a slice of bread and top with another slice of bread.

   This is a nice entree to serve for HONEY'S PEACEFUL DINNER (see page 492) but don't be reading a library book while you are eating it; the egg melts the butter and you'll get greasy finger prints on the book when you turn the pages.

FRIED PORRIDGE
contributed by Ma Trotter

Ingredients:
left over porridge (see REAL PORRIDGE on page 647)
butter
assorted toppings

1. Pack left-over porridge into a greased loaf pan and chill over night.
2. Remove porridge from pan and cut into one inch thick slices.

3. Melt butter in a frying pan.
4. Fry porridge slices in the butter until golden brown and crispy.
5. Serve with brown sugar, jam, or maple syrup.

CRUNCHY HOT DOGS
contributed by Lynnette Trotter

Ingredients:
wiener
bun
mustard, ketchup, relish, etc.
potato chips (any flavour)

1. Boil or fry wieners, or roast over a campfire.
2. Put the wiener in the bun and fix it up the way you like it.
3. Tuck potato chips in around the wiener, as many as you can pack in.

SURPRISE SOUP
contributed by Fudgie Trotter

1. Close your eyes and reach into the cupboard where the canned soup is kept.
2. Bring out two cans.
3. Open the cans and mix the two kinds together and heat according to the directions.

QUICK AND EASY BREAD PUDDING
contributed by Ma Trotter

Ingredients:
white bread
milk
raisins, nuts, chocolate chips, jujubes, etc. (optional)
assorted toppings

1. Rip the bread into large chunks and place in a bowl.
2. Add any or all of the optionals.
3. Pour on milk to moisten.
4. Top with maple syrup, jam, brown sugar or honey.
   For a richer taste you can use tinned evaporated milk.

HELPFUL HINT
contributed by Lynnette Trotter

TESTING FOR DONENESS: When you are cooking spaghetti you can test for doneness by breaking off a short piece of spaghetti and throwing at the ceiling. If it sticks the spaghetti is ready to eat. If you like your spaghetti *al dente,* test it by throwing it at the wall; if it sticks it is ready. This works for pork chops, too, but not if they are breaded.

Egg Nog

FOR A WHILE IT HAD LOOKED like they'd have to spend Christmas Eve in town, camping at Vonnie's mom and dad's. They'd been in town when the temperature dropped and the wind came up. By supper time of that day, snow was falling sideways at sixty miles an hour.

"You're not heading out into the wilderness in this weather, Vonnie," her mother had declared, "You and Ivor are going to spend Christmas with us."

"We kind of had our hearts set on spending our first Christmas in our own place, Mom," Vonnie said, "You understand. . . ."

"I understand that you aren't going anywhere if this weather keeps up! And that's final!"

Well, the weather kept up . . . until sometime early on the morning of the 24th. Christmas Eve day, the sun rose to drizzle its soft yellow light like butter on a mashed-potato town, and people started thinking about turkey.

"The weather's broke," Vonnie said to her mom, "I know you'd like us to stay, but Ivor and I agree that we'd really like to get home for Christmas."

"The roads are going to be pretty bad," cautioned her mom.

"Ivor's used to driving on snowy roads, Mom," Vonnie assured her, "We've got chains, and we've got a shovel. And we've got an extra couple of pairs of long underwear. We'll be just fine."

"Well, if you insist on going, let me give you a few things to take along."

Yvonne and Ivor left New Totem mid-morning with a box of food and drink sitting on the seat of the pick-up between them. A C.A.R.E. package Vonnie's mother called it — Christmas cake, two feet of summer sausage, a carton of egg nog, a plate of short bread cookies covered with tin foil, a can of cranberry sauce. . . .

"I'm not cooking a turkey, Mom. We don't have an oven." "Put it on the summer sausage," said her mom.

. . . two loaves of homemade bread, and a bottle of red wine with a packet of spices tied around its neck.

"You can make yourself some mulled wine to warm yourself when you get home. . . ."

They got stuck twice just getting out of town — the roads were that bad.

"The highway will be better," said Ivor, "More traffic."

The highway was better, but the Quarter Mile River Road was worse. Ivor was used to driving on snowy roads though, and Vonnie did her part — her part was not yelling at him no matter how close they came to sliding into the ditch or colliding with an oil delivery truck — she did her part, and by late afternoon they got to Clayton Summer's place at the Quarter Mile River. There was a road of sorts along the river and up Lynx Creek to the cabin, but they didn't bother trying to keep it open in the winter; they just parked the pick-up at Clayton's place and walked the five miles in.

"Clayton's not home," said Ivor, "He must have gone to his sister's place for Christmas. Let's get these groceries into our packs, and with a little luck, we'll still get to spend Christmas Eve at home."

So late on the afternoon of Christmas Eve of their first Christmas together as man and wife, Ivor and Yvonne Dressler strapped on their snowshoes and set off swish-clomping along the Quarter Mile River toward the little cabin on Lynx Creek that they called home. Late afternoon is pretty well early evening on the Vast Northern Prairie, so it was already getting dark when they started off through the willows along the river flats. By the time they got to the place where that big spruce had fallen across the path, it was early evening, which is to say that, in terms of dark, it might as well have been midnight. There were some stars out though, and the white of the snow picked up their glow and spread it around so it didn't really seem dark at all.

"Ivor, what's that light off to the right?" Off to the right, a ravine cut a gouge way back into the hills. During break-up there was quite a little creek pouring down the ravine, but it dried up about the middle of June. "No one lives up there. What could it be?"

"It's a star shining, Vonnie," said Ivor, "It's low down in the sky. . . . "

"No, Ivor," said Vonnie, "It's too bright for a star. Could it be the Forestry look-out tower. . . ."

"You can't see that tower from here, Vonnie. And besides, the Forestry people don't keep the tower open in the winter. That's just a star shining, I tell you."

"Well, it doesn't look like a star to me," Vonnie insisted, "What if someone's lost out there. Maybe a plane went down. . . ."

"You're not going to be happy till we go and check it out are you, Vonnie," said Ivor.

"I would make me feel better, if I knew for sure."

They turned away from the Quarter Mile and headed up the creek bed toward the light. It was hard to judge distance in the snow light, but it seemed like they'd gone at least a mile or more when the ravine widened out into a flat bench of land. That's when Yvonne spotted the light again.

"It seems high up, alright," said Vonnie, "Maybe someone's built a place on top of the hills. . . ."

"We should be able to tell soon enough," said Ivor. "We'll go a ways further."

A ways further along, Vonnie stopped still.

"Listen, Ivor. Can you hear it?"

"Sounds like somebody crying. . . ."

"Sounds like a baby crying, Ivor. And that's what it is. Come on."

A couple minutes later, they saw the breathless yellow light of a coal oil lantern shining through the dark.

"I think I can see a little cabin up ahead," said Ivor, "And that's where the crying is coming from."

He shuffle-shuffled off toward the light. Yvonne stood a moment watching him go, and, watching, realized that the light from the cabin window wasn't what had drawn them away from their path. The light was shining soft and wobbly from the window, but a stronger light was shining above. Ivor was right; it was a star and it was shining right above where the cabin was and right where Yvonne had never seen a star before.

"But I'm no astronomer," she said to herself. And she ran to catch up with her husband.

The man's name was Joe. He was quite a bit older than Ivor or Yvonne. There was a lot of grey in his long beard, and a lot of shiny forehead running back from his great shaggy eyebrows. The baby had a face like a bright red prune and a good set of lungs.

"He's only about four hours old," said the man, referring to the squalling bundle in his arms, "but already he's worn his mom out. Maryanne gave him the breast right away, and he just wouldn't quit sucking. About an hour ago, she gave him to me, 'You look after him,' she said, 'I'm going to sleep.' He doesn't like me though."

The baby's mom was sound asleep under a patchwork quilt on a rough bed in the shadows at the back of the single room.

"Could be he's hungry," suggested Ivor.

"Doesn't seem likely after he's been nursing for three hours," said Joe.

"Do you have a bottle and some milk," asked Yonne. "It wouldn't hurt to offer him some. . . ."

"We've got a bottle, but nothing to put in it," said Joe. "We ran out of milk, and he's bit young to be drinking coffee. . . ."

"How about the egg nog," said Ivor, "I wonder if he'd like egg nog?"

"That might be a bit rich for a new baby," said Yvonne, "I don't know. . . ."

"I don't know what else to do," said Joe, "Let's give him a bit, and see how he likes it."

So they got the carton of egg nog out of the pack and poured some into the baby's bottle. He liked it alright. Yvonne sat and rocked him and cooed to him, and he drank the whole thing.

"I think he's gone to sleep," whispered Yvonne.

"I'll take him and lay him with his mom," whispered Joe.

"It's okay," whispered Yvonne, "I like holding him."

While Yvonne had been feeding the baby, Ivor had taken the rest of Yvonne's mother's C.A.R.E. package out of their packs and set it out on the table. Joe'd provided an aluminum sauce pan and now the wine was mulling on the airtight heater, and the little cabin was sparkling with the smell of it.

"Help yourself to some bread and sausage, Joe," said Ivor, "You like some wine, Vonnie?"

The baby's mom woke up and set herself up on one elbow.

"I could use a cup of that wine myself," she said, "if there's some to spare."

So they sat there in the soft light of the lamp, listening to the coals pop in the heater and to the baby breathing, and they ate shortbread cookies and Christmas cake, and they talked a bit.

"Oh, I'm not the baby's father," Joe told them, "I'm just a friend. Lloyd just asked me to bring Maryanne out to meet him. We'd expected him before this, but we've learned not to worry where Lloyd's concerned. He'll be here in his own good time."

Maryanne was sitting cross-legged on the bed now with the quilt pulled over her shoulders and the baby sleeping in her arms.

"Ivor and I live just down on Lynx Creek," Vonnie said to Maryanne, "Looks like we'll be neighbours. . . ."

"I'd like that," said Maryanne, "but Lloyd might have plans."

"Lloyd's a great planner," said Joe, "but he's not so great at letting other people in on his plans sometimes."

"Well, we'll see then. . . ." said Yvonne.

"Vonnie and me should be going soon," said Ivor, "We'll leave you the rest of the egg nog for the baby, and you can have the other loaf of bread and that last six inches of sausage. We'll come over tomorrow and see how you're doing."

"Thank you," said Maryanne. "We appreciate that. Don't worry about us though. Lloyd's coming."

Yvonne and Ivor put on their coats and mittens and paused uncertainly by the door.

"You're sure you'll be alright for tonight?" said Ivor.

"We'll be fine, Ivor," said Joe. "You and Vonnie have a nice Christmas."

He stuck out his hand, and they took turns shaking it. From the bed, Maryanne gave a little wave. They both waved back and then turned to go. As Ivor opened the door, Vonnie turned back again.

"By the way, Maryanne," she said, "what are you going to call the baby?"

"I don't know yet," said Maryanne. "I'll have to talk it over with Lloyd when he gets here."

The next day Vonnie and Ivor packed a few groceries in their packs and headed back up that ravine. The wind had sifted snow into the tracks that they had left the night before, but they had no trouble finding their way back to the cabin.

"But this can't be the right place, Ivor. . . ."

A good part of the roof had fallen in and the windows were empty squares. The sill crumbled under Ivor's boot as he stepped through the doorless gap in the wall. Snow was piled on the bed and dead weeds poked out of the rusted body of the stove.

"You're right, Vonnie," he said, "No one's lived here for years. . . ."

"Ivor, look at this," said Vonnie. She was standing by the table which was littered with odds and ends of books, papers, kitchen utensils, and animal droppings. In her hand was a waxed cardboard carton.

"It's an egg nog carton," she said, "It was here on the table."

Ivor stepped closer and looked down at the junk on the table. He picked up a rusted knife and turned it in his hands. He set it down again and picked up a paperback book that had been chewed all along the spine, and when he did a piece of paper that had been lying under the book lifted and slid down the still air onto the floor. Vonnie leaned over and picked it up.

"There's writing on it, Ivor," she said. "It says . . . 'We called him Travis.'"

She looked at her husband with questions dancing in her eyes.

"That's a good name," said Ivor.

Toad Spring

TOAD SPRING — YOU SOMETIMES HEAR that term toward the end of a long winter up on the Vast Northern Prairie.

You might hear Lyla King say to Dora Ritter, "I wouldn't be planting out those onion sets quite yet, Dora. Weather's been nice the last few days, but I got a feeling it's just Toad Spring."

Toad Spring is kind of the same thing as Indian Summer only the opposite, if you know what I mean.

"I wouldn't put away my parka just yet, if I were you, Ma. Don't be fooled by a little spell of Toad Spring."

Sometimes you'll get a few days of really nice weather late in the winter — feels just like spring — but then winter closes in worse than ever for a week or a month. That warm spell is what they call Toad Spring, and I'll tell you why they call it that.

Years ago there was a kind of toad that lived in the hot springs up along the Liard River. These toads looked like big brown rocks and smelled like sulphur. And they were hot to the touch. People used to argue about whether the toads were hot from living in the hot pools or the pools were hot because those hot toads were living there, but the toads are gone now and the pools are still hot, so I guess they weren't hot on account of the toads.

There were thousands — maybe millions — of these hot sulphur toads living in the pools that are fed by the hot springs along the Liard there, but one winter every single one of them headed south.

It was a particularly cold winter that year, and maybe, despite living in the hot water like they did, they got a chill and decided to look for a warmer home. In any case, they packed up and went south, every single toad in a great steaming crowd hopping south along the highway.

They moved at night and at first they moved pretty fast. When they hopped past Fort Mellon, they were going so fast, in fact, that people didn't even know that they'd been and gone. Pretty well everyone in town was at the hockey game the night the toads went through, and all they knew was that one minute the players were skating on ice, the next minute they were up to their ankles in water and the next minute the water was frozen again and both teams were stuck solid in the ice. The toads had come and gone that fast.

Everywhere the toads passed, it got to be spring for at least a few minutes. The souther they got, the slower they went, and Toad Spring lasted for a few hours in some places and a few days in others. And a lot of people got fooled.

Dougie Spencer and Sally White were planning to get married in the spring and when the toads hopped through town, they headed off down to the church. They got married alright, but by the time they came out it was winter again, and they had to cancel their honeymoon. They'd planned to spend a week camping and fishing on Lake Charles, but there was no way Sally was going camping in three feet of snow.

Arnie Dewhurst was cutting a siesmic line through the bush when the toads went by and thawed the muskeg right out from under him. Arnie jumped off the Cat just in time. The Cat sank out of sight, but Arnie was saved. He was in a pretty bad way by the time he got back to camp though. The first part of the way, he got mauled by the black flies, and then the winter hit again and he almost froze.

When the toads hopped by north of New Totem and Toad Spring hit the town, Stan Walsh went right out and took the snow tires off his car. Two days later it was the dead of winter again, and Stan's new car slid through the intersection at 100th Street and 99th Avenue, swerved up onto the sidewalk and knocked Maurice King through the front door of Totem Gifts.

Dora Ritter planted out her onion sets too soon, and they all froze.

Ma Trotter launched into her spring cleaning when the toads came by and lived to regret it. She was washing the outside of the kitchen window when winter hit again. The wash rag froze right to the glass, and Ma to the rag. Lynnette had to heat water in the kettle and dribble it down the glass to thaw out the rag and get Ma unstuck. After that Ma never started her spring cleaning till August at the earliest.

In a fit of Spring Fever, Ross Byers finally got up the nerve to ask Olive Rigley if he could walk her home from school. Olive agreed, but by Monday it was winter again, and when it was really cold Olive's mom always came with the car to pick her up from school. Olive's mom offered to give Ross a ride, but he said, "No, that's okay," and froze his left ear walking home.

Ross Byers wasn't the only wildlife to get fooled by the sudden spring. The black flies and mosquitoes rose up in clouds.

All the birds came back from down south and then had to turn around and fly right back again.

Bears came out of hibernation. When the cold weather hit again, they started grubbing around looking for a snack before they went back to sleep. There wasn't much out in the bush, so half a dozen of them tromped into town and ate all the honey and frozen blueberries at the IGA store. They ended up sleeping the rest of the winter in the empty refrigerator cartons out behind Walsh's Home Furnishings.

That little patch of Spring Time moved on down the foothills and into the United States. The farther the toads hopped, the cooler they got until, by the time they got to Texas, they were as cool as cucumbers if cucumbers were lumpy and brown. You couldn't tell them from ordinary toads except for the smell.

They found themselves a little corner of a swamp right on the Gulf of Mexico and that's where they're living now. If you're ever in Texas, you can go and smell them if you like. They still smell like sulphur.

Crossing South

Aʀɴɪᴇ ᴄᴀᴍᴇ ᴀᴄʀᴏss ᴛʜᴇ ᴡᴏʀᴅ in the "Improve Your Word Power" section of the *Reader's Digest:* pontaviasudaphobia — the fear of crossing bridges while travelling in a southerly direction. When he read that word, a little switch went click in his brain, and a tiny light bulb came on just like in a cartoon. By the light of that little bulb, one curious conversation and several strange stories became visible in a way that they had never been visible before.

Arnie put the *Reader's Digest* face down on the table, took a sip of his coffee, and reached for the phone.

"Doreen," he said, "remember when you and Angela just about got killed by that load of pumpkins? You said you'd picked up a hitch-hiker just before that happened. Do you remember what he was wearing?"

Doreen was Arnie's sister, and she and her daughter had been up from Carson's Creek to an auction in New Totem that day in late October. They came by the trailer for tea in the afternoon and headed for home about three o'clock.

They got to Tailor's Flats and were driving along that long straight stretch past the hotel when they saw a guy standing by the side of the road with his thumb out. Doreen stopped and the guy came running up and opened the passenger side door.

"Where you heading?" Doreen asked him.

"South," he said, "Across the bridge."

"Hop in then," said Doreen.

And Angela scooted over to make room for the guy.

Doreen checked the rear-view mirror and waited for a big red farm truck to go by them before she pulled back out onto the highway. A minute later they were following the truck through that little cut and down that bit of a grade heading onto the Peaceful River Bridge.

They were about halfway across the bridge when Doreen heard a terrible cracking noise and the whole back end of the truck they were following seemed to fly apart. Suddenly, all Doreen could see was this gigantic orange ball flying straight for them. She slammed on the brakes, but it didn't help. That monster pumpkin bounced once on the hood of the pick-up and crashed right through the windshield.

Doreen felt the pick-up come to a smushing stop, and all she could think of as she clawed pumpkin guts off her face was, "Angela! Is Angela okay?" When she'd got her eyes cleared she looked around. And she started laughing. She couldn't stop. Angela was standing out beside the truck with her eyes big as saucers and the top part of a pumpkin shell sitting on her head, the stem sticking straight up.

"Are you okay, Mom?" Angela said.

But Doreen couldn't stop laughing long enough to answer her, and Angela got scared and started to cry. Eventually, things got sorted out. Doreen stopped laughing and Angela stopped crying, and only then did Doreen remember about the hitch-hiker.

She asked the truck driver and the constable who came along to fill out the accident report, but nobody'd seen him. The constable wrote down a description, but Doreen never heard if they'd ever found him.

Arnie remembered that he'd heard another story a couple of

years before that about an accident on the bridge. Gary Hudson almost got killed in that one. There was a lot of wet snow on the road, and Gary met an oil tanker coming too fast the other way. Gary got blinded by slush kicking up from the tanker's wheels and he panicked. He swerved into the guard rail. He was in a coma for a couple of weeks and when he came to, he kept asking about a hitch-hiker that he'd picked up. Gary was the only one in the car when the ambulance arrived, so people just assumed Gary had been dreaming. That had been late in October, too.

And just last year, about the same time of year, the Clarkson boy had been killed on the bridge. As far as anyone could tell, his car had conked out, and he was getting out to go for help when someone came up too fast from behind and ran into him. They never found who hit him, and, of course, there was no reason to assume that there would have been a hitch-hiker along, but. . . .

"He was just an ordinary guy," said Doreen, "Young. Had on a yellow hard hat and a green checked wool shirt. He was carrying a big silver lunch bucket."

The young fellow Arnie had seen by the railway underpass had been wearing a green checked wool shirt and yellow hard hat. He'd been carrying a big silver lunch bucket. His car was pulled off onto the shoulder of the highway, and he was standing with his thumb out.

"Thanks for stopping," he said, "My car just gave up the ghost on me. I was afraid I was going to be late for work. I work at the plant. You going that far?"

"I'm going all the way to Carson's Creek," said Arnie.

"Just as far as the plant would be great," said the young man, "Although, I should get down to the Creek and see my mom one of these days. . . ."

"It's not all that far," said Arnie.

"No, it's not that far. . . ." said the young man, "But . . . you know, it's the strangest thing. . . ."

The sun edged its way up over the low hills to the east and set the frost-sparkled stubble in the fields to twinkling.

"It's the strangest thing. . . ." The boy was going to tell him what was strange Arnie knew, but it might take a while.

"I know it's really stupid, but . . . the idea of crossing the bridge gives me the heeby jeebies. Weird, eh? I've started out three or four times to drive to Carson's Creek and when I get to the bridge, I just can't go any further. Weird, eh?"

"This come on sudden?" asked Arnie, "I mean, you must have crossed that bridge to get here from Carson's Creek?"

"It's a funny thing," said the young man, "The idea of crossing going north doesn't seem to bother me; it's just when I have to cross going back south again. It was like that with the bridge that crossed the creek back home. I never minded crossing heading into town, but I hated crossing back. I could do it though. I didn't like it, but I could do it. But this bridge . . . I don't know. . . ."

"Well, it's a bigger bridge," said Arnie.

"Maybe that's it. . . ." said the young man.

A week later, the suspension bridge on the Peaceful River collapsed. One man was killed — an employee at the Frontier Petroleum Plant who was on his way to Carson's Creek to visit his mother. They never did find his body. There was a picture of the bridge in the paper, but no picture of the man who was killed. Arnie was pretty sure, though, that it was the young fellow he'd picked up the week before at the railway underpass, and when he thought of it, he got little prickles on the back of his neck. Arnie was young enough that he hadn't met many dead people.

"Doreen," Arnie asked his sister, "do you remember what day

it was exactly that that accident happened on the bridge? The twenty-first? You sure?"

Arnie looked at the Co-op calendar stuck on the wall beside the phone. Today was October twenty-first.

"Thanks, Doreen," he said. "Don't forget about Brandi's birthday next week. We'll be expecting you."

The young man was there, standing on the side of the highway in front of the hotel. The big silver lunch bucket was by his feet, and he had his thumb stuck out.

Arnie pulled over and watched in the rear view mirror as the young man came running up. As the boy pulled the door open and bounced up onto the seat of the pick-up, Arnie was surprised at how ordinary he looked.

"Going south?" said Arnie.

"I'm going across the bridge," said the young man, and he didn't sound too happy about it.

"You sure you want to do that?" said Arnie. "You don't sound too happy about it. . . ."

The boy looked at Arnie with eyes full of pain.

"No," he said, "I don't WANT to cross that bridge. But I have no choice. My mom is real sick. They said she might die. I've got to go. . . ."

Arnie put the truck in gear and eased out onto the highway. A bit along, he swung onto the frontage road and started heading back north.

"Hey, mister!" cried the boy turning his head in a panicky way this way and that. "Where are you going?"

"There's another way," said Arnie. "Just sit back and relax. I'll see you get across the river. And you won't have to cross the bridge."

The young man sat back with obvious relief and didn't speak again until they were on top of the hill.

"I've been trying to get there." He was talking as much to himself as to Arnie, but Arnie listened anyway. "Something always happened though. I never did make it across the bridge. And I've been real worried about my mom. . . ."

They headed down the hill to the Beaten River. Arnie glanced over at his passenger as they approached the bridge, but the boy seemed calm enough. They rumbled across — heading east — and climbed the hill on the far side.

"A friend of my mom's called the plant and told the foreman it was an emergency and could he fetch me to the phone. This lady said my mom had had a heart attack or a stroke or something and could I come. I just washed off the worst of the grease. . . ."

He held up his hands and looked at the them. The knuckles and the nails were black.

". . . . and grabbed my lunch bucket and went. I was so scared about my mom, I didn't even think about the bridge until I was halfway across, and then I realized where I was and my heart froze in my chest. That same moment, a big wind came whipping down the valley, and the bridge started to buck. All that steel groaning and screaming . . . and then the cables started breaking — snapping and whizzing. And then the road was ripped across like it was made of tin foil, and the car went over. It twisted in the air and bounced once off a cement pier, and then I don't remember any more after that. . . ."

The low sun, dit-dotting though the bare trees made a crazy dancing light on the boy's face so Arnie couldn't make out what kind of look there might have been there.

"That was the first time I didn't make it across the bridge," said the boy. And that's all he said.

Arnie talked about how it was his little girl's birthday next week, and how he hoped to get some work for his Cat up on the Quarter Mile soon and how, if he got enough work, the family would go to Disneyland for Easter. But the boy just sat there looking out the window, and Arnie stopped talking and drove.

The sun was down and the sky and the land were all leeched grey by the time they started down the hill above Clayhurst, and it was dark when they got to the bottom. Ten minutes later and they'd have missed the last ferry, but they made it with a bit to spare. The boy stayed in the truck, but Arnie got out and stood on the deck. The guide cable groaned as the black water growled around the steel hull of the little boat and tried to push them down to the Arctic Ocean. The old diesel coughed and muttered. A bit of a wind snatched at Arnie's cap and dragged his breath away into the night. But nothing bad happened, and they got across fine.

"No reason we shouldn't," Arnie said to himself as he got into the cab and started the engine. "A ferry ain't a bridge, even if it is going south."

Once they were across the river, the boy slumped against the door and fell asleep. He slept all the rest of the way into Carson's Creek. When they got to the Esso station at the edge of town, Arnie had to shake the boy hard to get him to wake up.

"We're there," he said, "Where would you like me to let you off?"

The boy blinked and rubbed his face. He looked around and had to think for a minute before he figured out where he was.

"This is okay right here," he said. "This will be fine."

"You sure?" said Arnie.

"Yeah," said the boy. He looked hard at Arnie.

"Thank you," he said, "I appreciate the lift."

"No problem," said Arnie.

The boy opened the door and hopped down to the ground. He picked up his lunch bucket from the floor and with a little wave, swung the door closed. Arnie waved one last time as the boy started down 89th Street toward the bridge that crossed the creek. Arnie glanced at his watch and decided it probably wasn't too late to drop into his sister's place for a cup of tea. He pulled up to the pumps and filled the pick-up's tank with gas and a few minutes later was turning onto the street again. He looked down 89th Street and saw the boy standing in the circle of light from a street lamp at the end of the bridge. As Arnie watched, the boy squared his shoulders and started walking. He stepped out of the circle of light and was swallowed up by the dark.

The Talking Meter

THE TOWN OF NEW TOTEM was the first town on the Vast Northern Prairie and perhaps in all of North America to install a system of talking parking meters. And that was nearly half a century before talking vending machines and talking cars had become a commonplace. This is how it happened.

The town of New Totem had put in twenty parking meters along 100th Avenue that summer, but no one was using them. Rather than pay a nickel or risk getting a parking ticket, people just parked one street over and walked.

The following winter, Danny Tomson won first place in the Bevin Williams Junior Secondary Science Fair with a talking gumball machine. When you put a penny in the gumball machine and turned the handle, the action released a gumball, but also closed a switch that activated the arm of a record player. The arm was rigged in such a way that it played the chorus of Roger Miller's big novelty hit "Chew That Thing — 'Chew, chew, chew that thing, Chew, chew, chew that thing. Etc.'" Kids were lined up out into the hallway waiting for a turn to put in their pennies.

Tomson's science teacher, Rafe Bunbury, was also on town council and, as luck would have it, was the head of a two-person committee charged with figuring out what to do about the town's idle parking meters. When he saw Tomson's Science Fair project, he instantly recognized how the technology could be applied to the parking meter problem.

The following Monday, he proposed to town council that they wire the parking meters up to record players that would play a little song or say something like, "Thank you for you nickel, friend. Remember to be back in half an hour." He brought Tomson's gumball machine along to show the council and talked about how popular the gizmo had been at the Science Fair. The other council members were quick to point out that it was going to cost a lot of money to buy twenty record players even if they were real cheap ones.

The next Monday, Bunbury came back with a modified proposal — hook all the meters up to one record player that would be hooked into a big loud speaker that would be installed on the roof of the Co-op Store.

Council passed the motion, and Bunbury and his committee were allotted seventy-five dollars to get the system up and running.

A month later, Bunbury parked his pick-up in front of the Co-op Store and put a nickel in the parking meter. A few seconds later, the chorus of Cindy-Lou Pratt's big hit, "Let's Park!" was booming down the street.

The townspeople flocked to 100th Avenue and cruised around the block waiting for a chance to park and listen to a bit of Cindy-Lou Pratt booming out from the roof of the Co-op. Rafe Bunbury drew up plans and applied for patents on a whole series of talking machines — talking washing machines for laundormats, talking newspaper vending machines, talking mail boxes.

Within a week, though, people got tired of hearing the same bit of the same song over and over again, and started parking one street over like they had before the talking parking meter system was installed.

Town council asked Bunbury to write up a report saying what went wrong.

Rafe Bunbury was mystified. Danny Tomson's talking gumball machine had been set up in the cafeteria and was just as popular as ever. Why would kids line up to put pennies in a talking gumball machine when their parents wouldn't put money in a talking parking meter?

The afternoon of the Monday that he was to make his report to council, Bunbury was sitting in front of the class supervising a chemistry test when the answer came to him. He looked at the class and saw forty teenage jaws moving in rhythm — chew, chew, chew. . . .

That night Bunbury addressed the council yet again on the problem of the parking meters. The council allocated a further fifty dollars to Bunbury and his committee — to dismantle the talking parking meters and install two prototype gumball parking meters. The new machines which gave you thirty minutes of parking AND a gumball were an immediate success, and the parking meter system paid for itself within a year.

Bunbury threw out all the talking machine plans that he'd made, gave up teaching and bought into a vending machine business. He lived to see talking machines become a multi-million dollar business and must have said to himself a thousand times, "If only. . . ."

Too bad, Rafe. . . .

The Ice Cream
Bucket Effect

Andrew Trotter was sitting in the driver's seat of the 1965 Dodge Valiant with his hands at ten o'clock and two o'clock and sweat dribbling down his sides.

"Now we've gotten through the basics. We've covered starting the car, and putting it in gear, going forwards, going backwards and stopping it again once you got it going. We've done hand signals and right and left turns. We've covered angle parking and. . . ."

"When are we going to practice beer bottle hucking, Mr. McLean?"

The driving instructor, Mr. McLean, turned his long body so he could face the two people sitting in the back seat.

"I told you, Olive," he said in a slow voice. "Beer bottle hucking is not part of the curriculum any more."

He turned his body back around and turned just his head so he could talk to Andrew's right ear.

"As I was saying. . . ." he said. "We've covered the basics, and if we could count on you kids having to drive only in basic situations, we could leave it at that. But we all know that situations will occur that call for more than simple basics. Take the ice cream bucket effect, for instance. That can occur in several different circumstances. You might find yourself driving in thick fog. You might have to navigate through a whiteout with snow blowing so thick and hard you can't even see the hood ornament. . . ."

"There isn't a hood ornament on this car, Mr. McLean." That was George Schecter, the other occupant of the back seat and the third member of the driver training class at Bevin Williams Junior High School.

Mr. McLean paused long enough to let George know that he'd heard and that he didn't intend to respond. And then he went on.

"But most likely the ice cream bucket effect will occur when you are driving in slush or mud. Here's a hypothetical situation. You're driving along, and the road is covered in six inches of slushy snow. A big truck hauling a load of culverts is coming toward you. As you and the truck meet, the truck sends a tidal wave of slush breaking over your windshield. Even assuming that you've had the foresight to turn your wipers on before this happens, it is going to take four or five seconds to get the windshield clear enough to see again. Now we're going to try that out in a controlled situation. We've got a straight piece of road here and not very much traffic. I want you to start the car, Andy, and start driving. Get it up to about forty, forty-five. . . ."

"I've got the bucket ready, sir!"

". . . . and when I give the signal, Olive will put that empty ice cream bucket over your head. At the same time George will start counting — one thousand, two thousand . . . like that. When he gets to four thousand, Olive will take the bucket off again. Okay?"

"Yes, sir."

"Now relax, Andy. This is just hypothetical, okay? Relax."

"Yes, sir."

"Well . . . start the car."

Andrew unclenched his hands from the steering wheel and wiped them on his pants. He reached up and turned the key in the ignition. He put his foot on the brake, and pulled the shift lever down until the little arrow pointed at the "D." He moved his foot from the brake to the gas pedal and the car lunged ahead.

The needle on the speedometer climbed past twenty and then past twenty-five. Andrew didn't see Mr. McLean give the signal, but, all of a sudden, Olive plunked the bucket down on his head and everything went white. He slammed on the brake. Andrew's head snapped forward and the bucket flew off. It bounced off the windshield, knocked the fuzzy dice off the rear view mirror and hit Mr. McLean in the face, before falling to the floor.

"That, Andy, is exactly what you DON'T want to do in a situation like this," said Mr. McLean. His tongue came out and touched the little stream of blood that was trickling out of his nose and collecting on his top lip. He leaned forward and opened the glove compartment.

"When you slammed on your brakes. . . ." he said, dabbing at the stream of blood with a Kleenex tissue, "when you slammed on your brakes, the hypothetical truck behind you smashed into your back end and killed you instantly. Does anyone in the back seat know what the proper procedure is to follow in a case like this?"

Both Olive and George stuck up their hands.

"George?" said Mr. McLean.

"We should call Mrs. Trotter and tell her that her boy is dead. Then we should dig a hole. . . ."

Mr. McLean spit on a new Kleenex and scrubbed away at his lip until George got through exlaining about saying "dust to dust" and filling the hole back in and tamping down the dirt and putting flowers on the grave, and then he said, "Olive, what do you think Andy should have done in this situation?"

"He should have eased off on the accelerator a bit, and just kept on driving as best he could until the windshield cleared again."

"That's right," said Mr. McLean. "The main thing is to not panic.

Ease up on the speed a bit, but don't do anything sudden — like slamming on the brake. We're going to try that again, Andy. Okay?"

"Yes, sir."

Andy slammed on the brakes again on the second and third attempts, and on the forth he steered them into a shallow ditch.

"That's better," said Mr. McLean. "You're getting it."

The fifth and sixth times he did it more or less correctly, but by that time George was getting bored with counting and was counting by twos and leaving out the "thousand" so it was a bit easier.

"Okay, let's let Olive have a turn," said Mr. McLean.

"If I do it right the first time can we practice beer bottle hucking?" Olive pleaded, "Please, Mr. McLean."

"That isn't up to me," said Mr. McLean. "The Board decided to cut that part of the curriculum, and I have to abide by that decision."

Only the week before, the Board had called a big meeting in the school gym and all kinds of people came out to discuss the issue.

"Kids are going to drink beer and drive," declared Ted Laboucan, "That's a fact of life. I used to do it myself when I was a kid."

"You still do, Ted!"

The crowd laughed, but Ted Laboucan just scowled at Harv Westaway and continued on with his speech. "Kids ARE going to drink beer and drive. That's the reason most kids even bother getting a driver's licence in the first place — so they can drink beer and drive. Now I'm not saying I approve of the practice. All I'm saying is — if they're going to do it anyway, it's our responsibility to teach them how to do it safely. If we take beer bottle hucking out of the driver training program, we'll have beer bottles bouncing off windshields and sailing through people's front windows. . . ."

"But isn't it against the law to drink beer and drive at the same time?" asked Dora Ritter.

"That's just my point," said Laboucan, "As soon as these kids see a cop, they're gonna huck those bottles out of the car, and if they aren't properly trained in the proper technique. . . ."

"Well, if it's against the law, I don't think we should be encouraging it by teaching it in school," said Dora.

Several of the School Board Members felt that Ted Laboucan had a strong argument, but when it came to the vote, beer bottle hucking was eliminated from the driver's training program.

So, even though Olive Rigley demonstrated great skill in coping with the ice cream bucket effect, and even though she wheedle most convincingly — "Ahhhh! My brother, Ken, got to do beer bottle hucking when he took the course." — Mr. McLean stuck to his guns.

"Let's give George a turn driving with the ice cream bucket on his head now."

In his dreams that night, Andrew Trotter found himself once more behind the wheel of that accursed Dodge Valiant driving at forty miles an hour through a featureless white fog. Any minute now, the car was going to plunge off a cliff or a hypothetical transport truck was going to smash into his back end — or his front.

"I hate it! I hate it! I hate it! Why am I doing this to myself? Why?" he muttered over and over. "Why? I won't do it anymore. No more!"

"What are you saying, Andy?"

Andrew looked over, and there in the passenger seat—it wasn't Mr. McLean with blood trickling out of his nose — it was Meghan! Meghan Spencer! She had curly red hair and lots of freckles. Some people might have thought that the glasses she wore with the heavy black frames made her look like one of the Beagle Boys from the *Scrooge McDuck* comic books, but Andrew thought they made her look intelligent.

"Are we almost home?" Meghan asked.

Ah, that's why he was doing it. That's why he was putting himself through this torture — so he could drive Meghan home.

"We should be there pretty soon," Andrew said. And he noticed that his voice sounded calm and strong. "It's hard to tell in this fog. Are your parents expecting you at any particular time?"

"Oh, no," said Meghan. "We could drive like this for ever, and I wouldn't mind. . . ."

Andrew tried to remember the message in the dream the next day as he sat there with his hands at ten o'clock and two o'clock listening to Mr. McLean talk about parallel parking.

"Chances are you'll never have to use it. Most towns around here have angle parking away. And if you're not particular about getting really close to where you're going — if you don't mind walking a bit — you can usually find a parking lot or a space on a side street where you've got three or four car lengths, and you can just wheel in. But the licence examiner will test you on it, so I'm going to teach it. Parallel parking! Okay, Andy, pull up by that pick-up, about this far away."

Mr. McLean held up his hands to show him how far.

"Good. Now listen. You're going to back up, Andy, and when the back bumper of the pick-up is about here, you're going to swing the wheel this way. You're going to keep backing, watching over your shoulder at the same time you're keeping an eye on your right front fender. Just keep backing, and when you're about lined up with the bumper of the car behind you're going to swing the wheel this way hard. You keep backing, and the front end will drop in behind the pick-up. . . ."

"If he does that too fast he'll hit into the truck, won't he, sir!"

"Yes, Olive."

"Do we have to pay if we crash the car, sir?"

"We've got insurance, George. But nobody's going to crash the car. Did you get that, Andy? Back up, turn this way, look that way and that way at the same time, keep backing, turn the other way, keep backing, and then you go forward a little until you're in the middle and you're done. Parallel parking! Got that?"

"Yes, sir. Can I put on the brakes if I need to?"

"Of course you can. . . ."

The next day they were supposed to practice moose avoidance techniques, but they weren't able to use Greg, the stuffed moose. The Loyal Moose were having a convention in Prince Charles that week, and they needed to take Greg with them, so Mr. McLean cancelled the moose avoidance part of the course.

"They don't usually test you on that," he assured them. "If it comes up, just tell the examiner that we couldn't get hold of the moose. He'll understand."

"Today we'll learn about washboard roads. You notice how this stretch of gravel road up ahead has little ridges running across it — like the ripples on an old fashioned washboard, right?"

"Yes, sir. . . ."

"That's why they call it washboard road. . . ."

"Yes, sir. . . ."

"Okay, start driving, Andy. Keep accelerating bit by bit. Not too fast, just bit by bit, and you'll notice something interesting."

At about fifty-three miles an hour, Andrew DID notice something interesting. His wheels were no longer touching the road. The car was floating. The steering wheel flopped around in his hand like a dead fish.

"I can't steer, Mr. McLean. It feels like the wheels aren't even touching the road. What should I do?"

"Don't panic, that's the main thing. It feels like your wheels aren't touching the ground because they're bouncing from ridge to ridge on the washboard so fast that for all intents and purposes they AREN'T touching."

"There's a curve in the road, sir. . . ."

The road curved, but the car floated straight off into the pine trees.

"Did you notice how fast you were going when it started feeling like your wheels were no longer in contact with the road, Andy?"

"I was going about fifty-three miles an hour, sir."

"Well, Andy, that's exactly how fast you should NOT have been going on a wash board road. And can anybody tell me how Andy could have avoided going that fast?"

"He could have slowed down," said Olive Rigley.

"That's right. . . . "

On Thursday they got the car stuck up to the axle in mud and practiced ways of getting it unstuck. They jacked it up and threw things under the wheel to increase the traction. They took turns bouncing up and down on the trunk. They pushed from the front, and they pushed from the rear.

"Just one little point about pushing from the rear," said Mr. McLean. "You notice how Andy's got a streak of mud running right up the front of him from his crotch to the top of his head? That happened because the back wheel has a tendency to spit out a stream of mud when it gets spinning. You're usually better off not standing directly behind the rear wheel like Andy was doing. . . ."

They finally ended up flagging down an Esso oil delivery truck.

The driver hooked a chain onto the frame behind the front bumper and pulled them out.

That night in Andrew's dreams, he and Meghan skidded and slipped and slewed through a hundred miles of greasy gumbo and didn't get stuck once.

Friday was the day for doing the theory part of the course. Olive Rigley didn't show up that afternoon. It turned out later that she'd gone off with her brother to practice hucking beer bottles. Lucky for her, she'd done so well on the rest of the course, because there was a test at the end worth fifty percent.

Andrew did really well. The questions were all multiple choice, and Andrew had always found that if he used a little common sense he could usually do pretty well on multiple choice.

George Schecter had his own theory about multiple choice questions. He figured that if you marked all the answers you were bound to get the right one.

George failed the course, and Olive only got fifty percent because she didn't show up for the theory part, so Andrew got top marks in the class and won a steak dinner for two at the Totem House Hotel.

He thought about asking Meghan Spencer to go with him, but the more he thought about it the nervouser he got. In the end, he went by himself and ate both steak dinners.

But as he finished off his second piece of pie, he vowed that in the fall, once they were back in school, and once he'd had time to practice a bit over the summer, he'd offer to give Meghan a ride home one afternoon. For sure!

The Rambler

WITH ONE THING AND ANOTHER, it was the middle of January before Andrew Trotter actually worked up the courage to offer Meghan Spencer a ride home from school.

One thing was — Andrew was shy around girls. Oh, he liked girls; he just couldn't see why one might like him. After a lifetime of listening to his mother and two older sisters talk about the men in their lives, the proposition seemed dubious at best.

Another thing was — the Rambler. There was no way he could offer a girl like Meghan a ride in a car like that Rambler station wagon. The Rambler was the Trotter family car. It was small, and it was baby blue, and if it started to rain on the way home, Meghan would have to hang out the window and pull on the windshield wipers to get them started. The ashtray was overflowing with cigarette butts and the back seat was a foot deep in empty potato chip bags, old overshoes, comic books, and don't even ask.

Andrew was no less shy by January, but he and Meghan had both been members of the chess club since October, and they'd exchanged enough pawns and mulled over enough chess problems together that he thought maybe she did like him a bit.

More importantly, though, the Rambler had developed some kind of problem with its clutch late in November. Dave down at Doug's Garage had had the thing apart and back together several times with no improvement. About the middle of December, he decided to send away for parts.

"I think it's the linkage, Marvin," he told Andrew's dad, "I'm gonna send away for parts."

Marvin was sceptical. That's what the mechanic had told him when the Monarch started burning oil. He suspected that sending away for parts was something mechanics did when they couldn't figure out what the problem was.

"How long is that going to take, Dave?"

"Depends. Maybe they got them in Carson's Creek. Maybe we'll have to send to Calgary."

"So what am I supposed to drive to work in the meantime?" said Marvin.

"Oh, we'll give you a courtesy car!" said Dave, "It's yours to use until the parts come in."

Well, the courtesy car was a beauty. It was a 1967 Pontiac Charger, sleek grey, without a single butt in the ashtray. And boy, was it powerful! Even when the chinook hit around Christmas and the driveway turned to muck, there was no way you could get that car stuck.

Marvin was working as a janitor on the afternoon shift at Bevin Williams Junior High, one block west of North Prairie Senior where Andrew went. Lately, Andrew had gotten in the habit of going over to the junior high to pick up the car to drive home, something he never did with the Rambler if he could help it. That meant he had to stay awake and go pick his dad up when he got off at 11:30, but Andrew didn't mind. He actually LIKED driving that sleek grey Pontiac!

So that Thursday afternoon, as he and Meghan were packing up the chess pieces, and the wind was curling the snow down off the roof past the windows and the temperature was dropping —

minus thirty-five and still going down — it all came together: a nice car, a cold day, and a girl who seemed to like him.

"Would you like a ride home?" he asked.

"I usually walk," said Meghan, "It's only a few blocks."

"It's cold out," said Andrew, "I could run over and get the car from my dad. It would only take a few minutes."

"Okay," said Meghan.

"Okay, good!" said Andrew, "Why don't you finish putting the game away while I go get the car. Let's see . . . I'll honk. I'll honk the horn and you come out."

"It's okay," said Meghan, "I'll just wait out by the street for you."

"Okay! Okay! I won't be long."

Andrew found his dad and the other two janitors sitting around the small table in the janitor's room drinking tea and Coffee Mate, waiting for the halls to clear so they could fire up the floor polishers and unsheath the razor blades that they used for scraping gum off. Marvin wiggled his hand into his pocket and pulled out the car keys. He handed them to Andrew. Andrew looked at the keys in his hand and his heart dropped. These weren't the keys with the tooled leather key ring. These were the ones with the cheap plastic key ring — the keys to the Rambler.

"You got the Rambler back?" said Andrew.

"Yep."

"Well, is it fixed?"

"Yes, it's fixed," said Marvin.

"Well, did they fix it properly this time?"

"It seemed to run fine," said Marvin.

There was nothing to be done about it then. Andrew couldn't very well give the keys back now.

He found the Rambler in the parking lot and unplugged the

block heater. He slipped into the driver's seat and shuddered as his backside hit the cold plastic. He put the key in the ignition. With a grinding like bone on bone, the starter motor laboured to turn the engine over. Andrew pumped the gas. The engine caught and started to scream in an aggrieved voice. Andrew backed off on the gas, and the engine settled into a resentful mutter.

Andrew felt around on the floor under his feet and found the window scraper. As soon as he took his foot off the gas to step out and clean the snow and frost from the windows, the engine stopped with a thud.

With a rueful shake of his head, Andrew turned off the ignition and got out of the car. He did a quick scrape of the windshield and the two side windows and got back in.

With a sense of dread, Andrew put the key in the ignition again. Reluctantly, the engine responded to the prompting of the starter motor. As long as he kept giving it a bit of gas, it seemed to be okay. If he backed off on the gas too far, the engine started to cough, so he kept a steady pressure on the accelerator.

Andrew looked at his watch. It had been over twenty minutes since he'd left Meghan. She was probably standing out in front of the school at that very moment slowly freezing to death and cursing him.

The air blowing out of the defroster vents was still blowing cold, but he figured he'd better go. He pushed in the clutch, shifted into reverse, and glanced over his shoulder to make sure there was nothing behind him. He gave the engine a little more gas and started to ease up on the clutch. The clutch didn't respond. Andrew looked down, and saw the pedal still sitting there against the floor mat.

"Must be frozen," Andrew muttered.

He hooked his toe under the pedal and gave it a nudge. The

pedal leaped off the mat, the clutch engaged, and the Rambler startled backwards like a pig that had brushed up against an electric fence. The engine stopped with a clunk.

Andrew shifted into neutral and started the sequence again. Again, the clutch pedal froze to the floor and stayed there till he nudged it up with the toe of his boot. Then it sprang up, the clutch engaged, the car leaped a foot backwards — and stalled.

"Okay . . . okay," he muttered, "Let's try this."

He got the engine going again, pushed in the clutch, and shifted into reverse. He pushed the gas pedal all the way down. The engine roared and when roaring didn't do any good, it whined. When it had settled into a six-cylinder impersonation of a jet engine warming up, Andrew nudged the clutch pedal off the floor. The car jumped back. It groaned deep in its oily soul as if mourning its lost youth. It took another jump, and another, and from somewhere in the depths of its subconscious dredged up the memory of reverse. It reversed across the parking lot and into a snow bank. And stalled.

Using the same strategy — gas pedal full down and pop up the clutch pedal — Andrew managed to get the Rambler to hop forward like an arthritic toad. After a few hops, it seemed to decide that it was just as easy now to keep going as to stop; and it kept going, the frozen tires thumping and the snow creaking as it limped its way out onto the street.

At the corner, Andrew executed a manouever that he remembered from driver training — a manouever known as a Hollywood stop — that allowed you to go through a stop sign without actually stopping as long as you were going slow enough that you could stop if you HAD to. He remembered learning that the manouever was not strictly legal, but he knew that if he brought the Rambler to a complete stop, he'd have to coax it through its crippled toad routine again. And that might work, and it might not. He executed another Hollywood stop at 104th Street and a third at 103rd, but eventually he was in front of the senior high, and he had no choice but to stop.

Meghan was there waiting on the sidewalk, clutching her homework books to her chest, and looking anxiously down the street. Andrew eased up as close as he could to the curb. Meghan kept looking anxiously down the street. In the time it had taken to drive from the junior high to the senior high, the insides of windows had frosted over completely except for a small semi-circle in front of the steering wheel. If Meghan even noticed the Rambler, there was no way she could see who was driving it.

Andrew knew that he should get out of the car. He knew that he should go over to Meghan and offer to take her books. He should escort her to the car and open the door for her. He should take her hand and help her into the car, and then shut the door.

But if he took his foot off the gas, the engine would stall. And it might not start again. No . . . better he stay in the car. . . . He called and waved, but Meghan kept looking anxiously down the street.He'd have to honk the horn to get her attention. He pressed the horn button as delicately as he could, hoping to produce a melodic "tootle toot" that would say: "Yoo hoo, Meghan! Over here, my dear." But that ill-mannered little automobile only knew one call, an unpleasant bleat that was at once aggressive and unimpressive. The Rambler bleated at Meghan Spencer.

Andrew squirmed with embarrassment as Meghan turned to look at the impertinent baby blue derelict that sat huffing at the curb. She bent over and squinted to see through the frost on the windows. Andrew waved, and very hesitantly, Meghan approached the car. She put her head close to the window and tried once more to peer through the frost. Andrew, fearing that she would turn and leave, leaned across and tugged down on the door handle. He gave the door a shove and it swung open eagerly, smacked into Meghan's forehead and knocked her glasses into the snow.

"I'm sorry!" Andrew mumbled. "I'm really sorry. Usually, the door sticks when it's cold. I didn't mean to push that hard . . . I couldn't get out because if I take my foot off the gas, the car stops. And there's something wrong with the linkage. It's stiff — the clutch linkage. It's frozen I guess. They were suppose to fix it."

Meghan got in and shut the door.

Andrew revved the engine to maximum, and they toad-hopped out into the street.

"You see what I mean about the clutch. . . ."

They approached 101st Street. There was too much cross traffic to risk a Hollywood stop, and besides Meghan might not approve. She was Catholic, and Catholics probably always stopped for stop signs. He brought the Rambler to a complete stop well back from the crosswalk.

"Could you scrape a little of the frost off that window so I can see if anything is coming?"

They hopped across 101st Street and chugged down past The Red Dragon Cafe — Chinese and Western Cuisine. Any hopes Andrew had of ever taking Megan there for the #2 Combination Plate were dead now. The best he could hope for was to get them across 100th Street without being run over by a truck.

There was 100th Street right ahead. Trucks were rumbling by in both directions, big trucks with great iron grills and huge, vicious-looking tires. These trucks didn't stop. With their loads of cement and steel pipe and heavy equipment, they always had the right of way. The billowing exhausts of all those trucks gave the scene a hellish quality, and Andrew Trotter sat writhing in his own little hell as those demon trucks roared by, daring him to make his move.

Andrew squinted out through his little peep hole in the frost at the frozen inferno that was 100th Street. He was poised and ready — the engine screaming and his toe hooked under the clutch pedal. Behind him, someone started to honk his horn.

"Is there anything coming that way?" he said, his voice barely a whisper.

Meghan spoke, but Andrew never knew if she said "yes" or "no." Suddenly, the clutch pedal came unfrozen and sprang up of its own accord. They were catapulted onto 100th Street and trucks were bearing down on them from both sides. The Rambler lurched forward, groaned in despair, and lurched again. It moaned and shuddered, and all at once, Andrew realized that the loathsome baby blue station wagon had chosen that moment to die. It was going to commit suicide right there on 100th Street in New Totem. And in doing so, it was going to sacrifice himself and the one girl who seemed to like him a bit. No way!

"Go!" he hollered. He punched his foot down harder on the gas pedal. He pounded on the steering wheel. The car shook itself and found the strength for one last leap. They were across 100th Street!

Andrew's foot was still shoved down hard on the gas pedal, so when the back tires hit an icy spot, they started to spin with a high screaming sound, singing in celebration or wailing in anger. Then the treads found a spot of dirty snow, grabbed on, and sent them hurtling forward into a fire hydrant.

The Rambler stopped with a clunk.

"I don't mind walking the rest of the way," said Meghan, "It's not far."

"Maybe that would be best," said Andrew, "If you don't mind."

"No," said Meghan, "I don't mind."

She pushed the door open and stepped out into the snow bank. "Bye, Andrew," she said.

When she slammed the door, the glove compartment flew open, and an avalanche of comic books and candy wrappers spilled onto the floor.

Games of Chance

ANDREW SLID HIS BANK CARD out of his wallet, checked that he was holding it the right way round and inserted it in the slot. Electronic fingers grabbed the card and whisked it away to the secret place behind the plastic wall of the Automated Banking Machine.

ENTER YOUR PERSONAL IDENTITY NUMBER AND PRESS *ENTER.*

Andrew did that.

The video display flinched and a list of options appeared glowing green next to the row of chrome buttons.

WITHDRAW -------- >
DEPOSIT ---------- >
BILL PAYMENT ------ >
TRANSFER --------- >

Andrew pressed the button beside the word *DEPOSIT* and fumbled his cheque out of his pocket.

TO WHICH ACCOUNT? the machine wanted to know.

CHEQUING --------- >
SAVINGS ---------- >
CREDIT CARD ------- >

Andrew selected *CHEQUING.*

ENTER AMOUNT OF DEPOSIT.

Five. . . . *bip!*   Zero. . . . *bip!*   Decimal. . . . *bip!*   Zero. . . . *bip!*
Zero. . . . *bip!*

This was a familiar sequence, not as familiar perhaps as the sequence used to withdraw cash, but one that Andrew had performed innumerable times.

That's why he stood there blinking for a few seconds before it registered in his brain that the machine had introduced a new topic of conversation. Instead of saying, PLACE DEPOSIT IN ENVE-LOPE PROVIDED AND INSERT ENVELOPE IN SLOT, the machine was asking him if he wanted to play.
WOULD YOU LIKE TO PLAY?
YES – – – – – – – – – – – – – – >
NO – – – – – – – – – – – – – – >

When Andrew didn't respond, the screen flinched, the speaker beeped impatiently, and the invitation danced back into view:
WOULD YOU LIKE TO PLAY?
YES – – – – – – – – – – – – – – >
NO – – – – – – – – – – – – – – >

The thought occurred to Andrew that he was being filmed by hidden cameras. He looked around self-consciously, and only then noticed the sign mounted on the wall next to the banking machine:
NEW! NEW! NEW!
INTRODUCING — LOTTOPOSIT
A NEW WAY TO WIN!
NEW! NEW! NEW!

"New?" thought Andrew. "That's not new is it? I'm sure I remember there was something like that when I was a kid. . . ."

When Andrew was a kid his family lived in the little town of New Totem on the far western edge of the Vast Northern Prairie, and New Totem was a town that loved to play.

In New Totem you could play regular Bingo any night of the week — on Monday at the Community Hall, on Tuesday at the Wolfendale Hall, on Wednesday in the gym of the Catholic School, on Thursday in the basement of the Lutheran Church, and on Friday at the Seniors' Home.

You could win a car playing Radio Bingo, and you could win a radio playing Bingo in your car while you were waiting for the drive-in movie to start.

You could play Bossie Bingo at the New Totem Fall Fair. They divided a big field into numbered squares. For five dollars you could purchase a square. When all the squares were sold they turned a well-fed heifer out into the field and waited for nature to take its course. If the heifer made a deposit on your square, you pocketed half the cash.

You could win free passes to the movies if the numbers on the gas pump matched this week's lucky number when you were filling up at the Royalite Station.

You could bet on the when the ice would go out on the Peaceful River in the spring.

New Totem had it's own version of Scratch-and-Win long before it became a commonplace in the rest of the country. You could buy a ticket for fifty cents and if you were the first person to come down to the newspaper with a mosquito bite in the spring you could win a year's supply of Deep Woods Off and a year's subscription to the *New Totem Gusher*.

You could play pool for money in the shadowy room behind Parker's Barber Shop or gamble for gold fish at the Friendly Pet Emporium and Flower Shop.

You could bet on the hockey games at the Civic Arena, the barrel races at the rodeo, or the Wheel of Fortune at the Fall Fair.

On any given evening, you could count on an average of three kids coming to the door with raffle tickets to sell. Ma Trotter won a prize on a raffle once. She bought three tickets for fifty cents from a boy who was raising money for a new stuffed wolf head for Cub Pack #11, and she won a trip for two to Edmonton — all expenses paid. She was pretty excited till she went to claim her prize and found out that it was a trip by dog-sled and you had to supply your own dogs.

In eighty-six percent of the houses in New Totem on any given evening, you'd find family and friends gathered in the kitchen to play Canasta, Hearts, Romoli, Monopoly, Aggrevation, or Croquinole — and never for less than a penny a point.

At the Legion the game of choice was Cribbage; at the beer parlour in the Totem House Hotel it was Shuffle Board.

Games of chance were as much of a part of daily life in New Totem as the wind and the sky.

Even getting your mail was a game of chance in that town. Celine Prowser, the Post Mistress, had been needing new glasses for years, but every time she got a little extra cash put aside, she'd end up losing it playing Croquinole.

"I can hit the other guy off okay," she said, "but sometimes I see two buttons when there's only really one there and half the time I shoot at the one that isn't there. . . ."

Well, the upshot of that was that Celine wasn't all that good at reading what was written on the envelopes and packages that came into the post office. She'd do her best, but the distribution of envelopes and parcels was accomplished as much by chance as by design.

At first people got upset and made a big fuss and went to considerable trouble to return misdirected items. After a while, though, the gaming spirit kicked in and, by some mysterious process of consensus, it was accepted that whatever showed up in your mailbox was yours to keep.

Ma got an electric massaging machine from Maurice King's mother for Maurice's birthday one year. And Dora Ritter's niece was already back from her honeymoon before Dora happened to run into Tammy Walsh at the Co-op, and Tammy told her about getting an invitation to the wedding.

"I'd never met your brother's youngest girl before," Tammy said to Dora, "but we had a wonderful time at the reception. . . ."

Ma Trotter's favourite game was Supermarket Bingo. Ma always bought a card to have when she went shopping for groceries. Across the top of the card there was a row of little pictures that represented the various sections of the store: a little carrot to stand for the Produce Section, a little cow for the Dairy Section, a little picture of a roll of toilet paper to represent the Paper Products Section, a little toothbrush for the Personal Hygiene Section, a little chicken for the Meat and Poultry Section and a silhouette of Mr. Peanut for the Nuts and Candies Section. Under each picture there were three square boxes.

When she was trundling a shopping cart around, Ma would hear a voice come over the loud speaker from time to time. It might say, "Under the carrot: 'W'," and Ma and all the other shoppers would go rushing off to the Produce Section of the store. They would rummage through the fruits and vegetables until one of them found the little plastic disk with the "W" on it.

If Ma got there first — and she usually did; Ma could move surprisingly fast for a woman her shape — and if she found the plastic disk first — which she often did — Ma would take the disk to the lady at the cash register and get a "W" stamped in the first box under the picture of the carrot.

A while later the voice might call out, "Under the chicken, 'N'," and the race would be on again.

The object of the game was to get all three letters — "W", "I",

"N" — filled in under a picture to win something free from that section of the store. Ma got WIN under the picture of the toothbrush one time and won a free box of denture cleaner. Another time she got WIN under the chicken and won some liver.

Given the New Totemites' passion for games of chance, it's not surprising that the local bank introduced an early version of LottoPosit back when the only thing automatic about the bank was the fact that it charged more interest than it paid. Each time you went to make a deposit you were given a chance to play The Cash In Game. If you decided to play, you wrote down a six-digit number on a piece of paper and gave it to the teller. The teller pulled six numbered ping pong balls out of a paper bag and wrote down the numbers. If four of your numbers matched four of the six that came out of the bag, you won ten times whatever amount you were depositing. If you didn't get four matching numbers, your money went right into general revenues.

After Marvin lost two pay cheques playing The Cash In Game, and the family ending up eating grilled cheese sandwiches for Thanksgiving dinner, Ma put her foot down.

"Marvin," she said, "we're moving our account to the Credit Union. You only have to match three numbers to win over there."

Andrew had had a bank account when he was a kid, but being a kid he wasn't allowed to play The Cash In Game. He could play LottoPosit, though.

He glanced around. No one was watching. He gave the machine a why-not look, shrugged his shoulders and put his finger on the *YES* button. The machine seemed to like that. The green display turned pink and delivered the message, "I AM OFFERING ODDS OF 100-TO-1 ON DEPOSITS OF $50.00 TODAY. YOU COULD WIN UP TO $5,000.00 IN DEPOSIT CREDITS ***INSTANTLY*** IF FOUR OF THE NUMBERS YOU CHOOSE MATCH THE NUM-

BERS CHOSEN BY THE COMPUTER. WOULD YOU LIKE TO
PLAY?

YES – – – – – – – – – – – – – – >

NO – – – – – – – – – – – – – – >

Andrew pressed the *YES* button.

ENTER A SIX DIGIT NUMBER. PRESS *ENTER* WHEN READY.
CORRECTION TO ENTER A NEW NUMBER. *CANCEL* TO
QUIT.

Andrew punched in the day, month and year of his daughter's
birthday. He pressed *ENTER*. The machine performed the electronic equivalent of pulling six numbered ping pong balls out of a
paper bag.

Not one single number matched the number that Andrew had
selected.

SORRY, YOU LOSE. BETTER LUCK NEXT TIME.

TAKE YOUR TRANSACTION RECORD.

The transaction record informed Andrew that $0.00 had been
deposited to his chequing account leaving a balance of $13.59.

DO YOU WANT TO DO ANOTHER TRANSACTION?

YES – – – – – – – – – – – – – – >

NO – – – – – – – – – – – – – – >

"No," said Andrew, "I guess not. . . ." He punched the button.

REMOVE YOUR CARD.

The electronic fingers slid Andrew's card back out through the
slot. Andrew took the card and put it in his wallet.

As he turned to leave, a man in a trench coat came through the
door.

"Tried out the new LottoPosit feature yet?" he asked.

"Oh yeah," said Andrew, "but I'll tell you; it may be a new
feature, but it's the same old game. . . ."

The Bent Owl of Quarter Mile River

Y OU'RE INTERESTED IN BIRDS?" said Arnie, "Well, I'll have to take you out to the Quarter Mile River to visit Clayton Summer and his bent owls."

"Bent owls?" said the school teacher. He WAS interested in birds, and knew a lot about birds, but he'd never heard of a bent owl. But then he WAS new to the area. "I've not heard of that particular breed of owl."

"Not many people have," said Arnie. "And fewer still have actually seen one. But Clayton has a whole family of them living in the rafters of his barn. Just by accident he found out that bent owls can't resist any kind of processed food. He was sitting on the chopping block eating a Spork sandwich one day. The phone started ringing in the house, so Clayton put his sandwich on the chopping block and went in to see who could be calling. When he came back out, there was this great big bent owl perched on the chopping block pecking the Spork out from between the slices of bread. As soon as the owl saw Clayton, he took off into the trees. But a couple of days later, the same thing happened with a Twinkie that Clayton was eating . . . phone rang, Clayton left part of a Twinkie on the chopping block, and when he came out, the same owl was tearing at it with his beak. Clayton's first thought was that he'd better take his food with him in future when he went to answer the phone. His second thought was, 'This owl sure seems to like the same kind of food I do; I wonder if I could tempt him with some Cheez Whiz on Ritz Crackers.' That's what Clayton was having for supper anyway, so he made a few extra and set them out on the chopping block. He watched through the window, and sure enough, the bent owl came swooping out of the trees and settled down to eat. Clayton kept feeding the owl whatever he was having — salted pretzels for breakfast and fried garlic sausage for lunch, and maybe potted meat and dill pickle sandwiches for supper. After about a week, the owl moved his family into the barn. The big daddy owl was still the only one that would come out, but Clayton would see him taking potato chips and chunks of Sara Lee cake up into the loft for the others. Clayton named the big daddy owl Monosodium Glutamate, but that's a bit of a mouthful, so most people just call him M.S.G for short."

"That's fascinating," said the school teacher, "And you think Mr. Summer would let me see this . . . bent owl of his?"

"Clayton loves to show off M.S.G. I have to head out that way Saturday morning, if you'd like to come along. You might want to pick up a box of salt and vinegar flavoured potato chips to bring. M.S.G tends to be a lot friendlier if you feed him."

Saturday morning Arnie drove the school teacher out to Clayton Summer's place where the road to Hunter's Bridge crosses the Quarter Mile River.

"Good morning, Clayton," said Arnie, "This is Brian Howe, the new school teacher. He's interested in birds, but he's never seen a bent owl. You think M.S.G. would come for a visit? Brian brought some potato chips."

"They only had dill pickle flavour left," said the school teacher, "They were right out of salt and vinegar. Will that be alright?"

"Dill pickle is M.S.G.'s favourite," said Clayton, "Just give me that box."

He ripped open the box, took out one of the two stay-fresh inner bags and ripped that open. He poured the green-tinged potato chips out onto the chopping block. He took out the other stay-fresh inner bag and opened that too. He offered potato chips to Arnie and the school teacher. Arnie said "No, thanks," and the school teacher shook his head.

"You're sure?" said Clayton. "M.S.G. should be along any minute, but you never know. We could be here a while. Can I get you anything at all? Carmel corn? You like something to drink? Coke?Lime Kool-Aid?"

Clayton had just finished the last of the greenish chips from his bag when a great grey shape came sliding out of the woods and feathered down onto the chopping block. The owl stood there on the block looking at them with his hard black eyes, one of which was quite a bit bigger than the other. One of his legs was little shorter than the other, too, so he tilted a bit to north. He had a little tuft of feathers over one eye — the big one — but not the other. The owl grabbed a dill-pickle-flavoured chip in one claw and snapped a piece off with his beak. He swallowed and swivelled his head to look at Clayton.

"You should get this kind more often, Clayton," he said, "They're my favourite. You know that."

"Mr. Howe brought them for you, M.S.G. He's interested in birds."

M.S.G. swivelled his head back and forth between Arnie and the school teacher, trying to decide which one was Mr. Howe.

"He's the one brought the chips," said Arnie, pointing to the school teacher. "He's a school teacher, and he's interested in birds."

The school teacher grinned and bobbed his head

"So, what do you want to know?" said M.S.G.

"I beg your pardon?" said the school teacher.

"You're interested in birds. I'm a bird. Ask me some questions."

"Well . . . ah . . . I . . . I usually just watch birds. I've never actually talked to a bird before," said the school teacher.

"You WATCH birds?" said M.S.G., "You don't talk to them?"

"I've never had the opportunity before. . . ."

"What kind of birds do you watch?" said M.S.G.

"Let's see. . . . Since I arrived in New Totem," said the school teacher, "I've had the opportunity to watch . . . crows . . . and whiskey jacks. . . ."

"Oh, yeah," put in Clayton, "you've got to watch whiskey jacks. They'll steal anything that isn't nailed down. Tom Ferguson had a goat once. . . ."

"Clayton," interrupted the bent owl, "The school teacher is talking."

"Sorry. . . ."

"So you've seen crows and whiskey jacks," said M.S.G., "Is that all?"

"Oh no," said the school teacher, "I've seen several other species as well. Chickadees. Woodpeckers. And several evening grosbeaks."

"Evening grosbeaks?" said M.S.G., "Evening grosbeaks are a dime a dozen. You seen any evening howjadoos?"

"Evening howjadoos?" said the school teacher, looking puzzled. He'd never heard of an evening howjadoo. But then, he'd never heard of a bent owl before either.

"Are they very rare?" he asked.

"You ever seen one, Clayton?"

Clayton shook his head. The owl looked at Arnie. Arnie shook his head, too.

"They must be pretty rare then, eh?" said M.S.G., "But I can show you where a whole flock of them live."

"You can?" said the school teacher. "That would be wonderful. When would be a good time?"

"How much cash have you got on you?" said the owl.

"I don't know. . . ." The school teacher pulled out his wallet and thumbed through it. "About forty dollars . . . and a bit of change."

"For a flat forty dollars, I'll take you right now," said the owl.

"Well. . . ." Forty dollars was a lot of money. But no other bird watcher that he'd ever talked to had reported sighting an evening howjadoo. He might get his name in the national bird watcher's newsletter, *The Twitter.*

"Alright," he said. He pulled three tens and two fives out of his wallet and handed them to the bird.

M.S.G. grabbed the bills in his beak and flew off toward the barn. The school teacher looked at Arnie with a question on his face.

"I imagine he's just gone to put the money in his nest," Arnie reassured him. "It would be foolish to go flying around in the forest with that much cash on you."

A minute later, M.S.G. was back.

"Just follow me," he said to the school teacher. He flew a ways and landed on top of a fence post.

"Come on!" he called back. A little hesitantly, the school teacher headed off after the bird. M.S.G. flew on a bit further and waited again, and then he did it again. Pretty soon, both the bird and the school teacher had disappeared into the poplar grove behind the barn.

A week or two later, Arnie ran into Clayton in the Marshal Wells store.

"That school teacher was out to see me again," Clayton told Arnie, "and he was pretty mad. He wanted his forty dollars back. I told him, 'I don't have your forty dollars. That's between you and M.S.G.'"

"They never found no evening howjadoos, eh?" said Arnie.

"No, no!" said Clayton. "That wasn't the problem. You see. . . ."

According to Clayton, the school teacher kept following the owl deeper and deeper into the bush along the river. By the time he decided that he'd made a mistake putting his trust in this bird, he was so deep in the bush that he knew he'd never find his way out again. He had no choice but to keep following on. M.S.G. kept him going all day, flying ahead a bit and waiting and flying ahead a bit and waiting. Late in the afternoon, the owl finally stopped at the bottom of a long ravine.

"Just follow that ravine up to where it levels out at the top," he said, "and you'll find all the evening howjadoos you'll ever want."

The school teacher nodded wearily. He didn't have the strength to say a proper *thank you*. He climbed up the ravine, and found himself at the end of the gravel road that runs into town past the lumber yard. He shuffled into town just in time to see the moon come sliding up behind the oil derrick in front of the Civic Arena.

He had to go right across town to where he lived on 111th Street, and as he shuffled along, people kept calling out to him, "Evening! Howjadoo?" "Evening! Howjadoo?" "Evening, Mr. Howe! Howjadoo?"

"When I told him I couldn't give him back his money," said Clayton, "he got REALLY mad. Before, he was pretty mad, but now he was REALLY mad. 'Where is that stupid bird?' he started yelling, 'I'm going to wring his neck!' And I said, 'M.S.G. isn't stupid. If you think he's stupid, don't ever get into a poker game with him. That's how Tim Lowell lost his farm.' But the school teacher wasn't listening, just kept on yelling about how if he just once got his hands on that stupid bird he'd do this and he'd do that. Finally, I brought him a bowl of cheese twists and that calmed him down a bit. 'M.S.G. isn't stupid,' I told him, 'M.S.G.'s an owl, and everybody knows that owls are wise. M.S.G.'s a bent owl though, and you've got to know this about a bent owl — a bent owl's wise . . . but he lies.'"

The next spring, Brian Howe went out to the Quarter Mile River to visit Clayton Summer once again. He had his cousin with him.

"Good morning, Clayton. This is my cousin from Edmonton. He's interested in birds. I was wondering if M.S.G. had time for a visit. My cousin brought a bag of potato chips — simulated ketchup flavour."

"I'm really sorry, Mr. Howe," Clayton said, "He left about six months ago, him and his whole family."

"Oh. . . ." said the school teacher, "Where did he go? Maybe. . . ."

"He went to work for Tommy Burnette," said Clayton.

"You mean THE Tommy Burnette?" said the school teacher.

"There is only one Tommy Burnette that I know of," said Clayton.

"Who's Tommy Burnette?" asked the school teacher's cousin.

"He was the mayor of New Totem for years," explained Clayton. "And then last election, he decided to run for parliament."

"Did he win?" asked the cousin.

"He sure did," said Clayton. "There's no way he could lose with a bent owl for a campaign manager."

The Trotter family in the Dew Drop Inn:
From left to right: Lynette, Honey, Pa, and Ma.
Andrew (Fudgie) and younger brother Patrick are in front.